GRACE ON THE MOUNTAIN TRAIL

CALL OF THE ROCKIES ~ BOOK 8

MISTY M. BELLER

Misty M. Beller
BOOKS

ISBN-13 Trade Paperback: 978-1-954810-51-8

ISBN-13 Large Print Paperback: 978-1-954810-52-5

ISBN-13 Casebound Hardback: 978-1-954810-53-2

Blessed is he that considereth the poor: the Lord will deliver him in time of trouble.
The Lord will preserve him, and keep him alive; and he shall be blessed upon the earth: and thou wilt not deliver him unto the will of his enemies.

Psalm 41:1-2 (KJV)

CHAPTER 1

EARLY WINTER, 1831
FUTURE MONTANA TERRITORY

A body lay sprawled beside the boulder.

A man. An Indian man.

Fear raced through Lola Cameron, and she gripped her rifle tighter but didn't raise it to aim. Was he dead?

If the man was alive, she didn't want him to think she meant harm. But she was ready if he sprang up to attack. Did Indian braves play possum?

He groaned and shifted as if trying to escape pain. He was alive at least, but injured or sick? Or perhaps too much strong drink.

And how had he gotten up here on the side of this mountain? She and her companions had seen no signs of others in the past day, not since leaving the plains for these low peaks that stretched along the edge of the Rocky Mountains. They weren't very far up the slope, but he didn't look like he'd come here under his own strength. Did he have friends nearby who would come back for him?

1

She scanned the length of him, starting with the disheveled black hair that covered much of his face, then over the white feathers tied in his braid, down his buckskin tunic and leggings, all the way to his moccasins.

Her gaze tripped there. What was that dark stain spreading across his lower leg? Blood?

"Lola?"

She jerked at the voice of the man approaching from behind her, then let out a steadying breath and settled her grip on the gun. Mr. VanBuren was supposed to be down the slope helping his son set up camp while she searched for extra firewood. With winter coming on quickly, the nights had grown frigid. Mr. VanBuren must have thought she'd been gone too long and grown worried.

She threw out her hand to slow his approach but didn't take her focus from the Indian, who'd shifted a bit more. "Look." She kept her voice low as she pointed to the stranger. "See his leg?"

Mr. VanBuren halted beside her, his breathing heavy from maneuvering the incline. "Who do you think he is?" He spoke as quietly as she had.

"I'm not sure. I thought he was dead at first."

"Hey, fellow. Who are you?" Mr. VanBuren called out in a gravelly bark that showed his advanced age.

The Indian didn't answer, nor did he move. But then, his leg shifted. It seemed he was trying to draw it into himself.

Lola couldn't tell if his eyes were open, thanks to the tendrils of hair mussed over his face.

Another groan drifted from him, not the loud obvious kind, like when a person pretended to be hurt. This one came from deep within, a soul-deep sound so guttural it barely reached them. If she were a betting woman, she would stake half their food on him being truly injured and not quite conscious.

"Are you hurt?" She spoke loudly enough for him to hear clearly across the dozen strides that separated them.

No answer. And no more movement from him. She started forward.

"Wait." Mr. VanBuren grabbed her arm. "Let me go first. Maybe we should call Will up here too. We might need both of us if this is a trap."

She eased her arm out of his hold. "I don't think it's a trap. Walk with me if you like." She motioned the older man forward even as she stepped out of his reach. She appreciated the source of his worries—concern for her—but she'd been caring for herself most of her life. She knew how to be careful, especially around strange men.

Mr. VanBuren crept along with her as they approached the Indian. When they'd closed half the distance, she could make out more of his face. Including the glistening of sweat and his pale bluish pallor.

And that leg. She still couldn't tell if the dark spot was blood, but it was definitely a liquid that had seeped through his leathers. A foul odor grew stronger the closer they drew.

She stopped just out of reach of the man. The way his shoulders heaved with each rasping breath made her own chest ache. She'd heard of wounds festering so much they made the person ill, but she'd never seen it herself.

Keeping a sturdy grip on her pistol, she stepped beside him and bent to swipe that hair from his eyes.

"Don't touch him." Mr. VanBuren tried to grasp her arm again, but she moved too quickly. Just because *he* was afraid didn't mean *she* had to be.

Even before her fingers brushed the Indian's skin, she could feel the man's heat. When she cleared the hair from his face, dark lashes brushed his cheeks. A bead of sweat trickled down his temple.

She glanced down his body. A knife hung in a sheaf suspended from his neck, and a tomahawk perched at his waist. His hands rested on the ground, not very near his weapons.

Every sign pointed to him being too ill to be a threat. Still, it would be wise to move the blades out of his reach.

After extracting the knife and tomahawk and tossing them away, she pressed her hand to his brow, both to feel its heat and to make her presence clear if his mind were foggy. "Can you hear me? Are you awake?"

His lashes fluttered as though trying to open, but they didn't. His mouth was parted only enough to draw in each hoarse breath.

Her own chest ached with his struggles. This man needed help.

She glanced around the little clearing. A boulder and a few trees blocked the wind from the south and west. This could do for their camp. It would certainly be easier than trying to carry this Indian down the hill to where Will was staking the horses.

She looked up at the man hovering beside her. "Can you yell for Will to bring our supplies before he unsaddles the horses? I think we'd better camp up here so we can help this man."

"Lola." Hesitation laced Mr. VanBuren's voice.

She worked to keep the frustration from her tone. "We can't leave him to die. We have to at least see what's wrong with him."

"I'm getting Will."

As Mr. VanBuren turned and called through the trees to his son, Lola shifted her attention to the Indian's leg. She needed to see what lay beneath that legging. Maybe removing the moccasin would show her enough, and she wouldn't have to cut the leather.

As she shifted down to his foot, the reality of what she was about to do nearly slapped her. She was touching a perfect stranger. *A man. An Indian.*

And she intended to remove his footwear. Women didn't do such things.

Yet, a glance at his face showed that his eyes remained

closed, his breathing still labored. Some situations required letting go of decorum. She could alert him before acting, though. "I'm going to take off your moccasin. I need to see your wound."

He didn't answer. Did that mean it was safe to proceed?

She had to lay her gun across her lap and use both hands to unlace the moccasin. With the leather spread apart, she could see the dark skin beneath. It held a deep purplish tint. Too dark, even for a native man.

She didn't have to remove the moccasin from his foot, for she could reach the bottom of his legging now. The stained area was in the middle of his calf, and the leather stretched tight around what must be significant swelling. The hem was loose enough that she could ease it upward a few inches.

As she did, more skin revealed a thick grayish liquid—the source of the foul stench. Her stomach turned, and she had to clamp her mouth shut to keep its contents intact.

The legging wouldn't rise any farther, not without tugging it across the wound. She reached for the knife she'd strapped to her waist. Even as she examined how best to maneuver the blade to cut the leather without slicing the skin, she had to strain to push away her dizziness.

There seemed no better option than to pull the legging away enough to fit the tip of her knife between the leather and the skin. She might bring pain, but it had to be done. For there to be any hope of helping the man recover, she had to clean the wound and douse it in salve.

She fit the tip of her blade against the buckskin.

"Lola, what are you doing?"

The sharp voice made her jump, and she glanced over her shoulder to see Will stomping toward her. He held his rifle with both hands, the stock tucked loosely against his shoulder and the barrel pointed at the Indian.

She braced herself over the stranger. "Don't harm him. He's injured and very sick. I have to cut this legging open to see how bad the wound is."

If Will VanBuren hurt him even more, she'd give him a taste of his own actions. She'd only met Will a few times before he and his father agreed to accompany her West, but he'd not been especially kind to the other Indians they'd met on the journey so far. Showing too much bluster didn't make friends of anyone.

He stopped beside her and used his boot to nudge the Indian's shoulder. He must have pushed hard, for the brave released another of those heart-wrenching moans.

She shooed Will back. "Can you make camp while I tend him? We're going to stay in this clearing." Usually she helped set things up and handled food preparation, even though she was paying both men to escort her through this wilderness.

Now, however, she had another task that needed her full focus. This Indian's life may well depend on her.

∼

*P*ain shouted to White Owl, summoning him out of the mist. He didn't want to face the torture, but he couldn't seem to resist its tug.

Little by little, the blackness receded as he moved toward the sliver of light.

Voices sounded around him. Was this one of his spirit dreams? But he'd turned away from those spirits. Did Creator Father also give visions? He'd had so little time with the missionaries. So many questions he'd not thought to ask.

Flames licked at his leg, and he struggled to pull it from the fire. To stop the searing heat.

The poke of red-hot metal scraped up his skin, and he could no longer hold in his cry. A voice sounded again—a woman's— and agony of the blade ceased.

He tried to hone in on her words, but it took several heart-beats of straining to clear away the buzzing in his ears. He could finally make out the sounds she spoke, but they didn't make sense. Not at first.

The white man's tongue. She wasn't speaking Shoshone. No wonder he'd had trouble understanding her. He knew a little English, but he didn't have enough energy to decipher her words.

Still, he tried. Forced his mind to find the cadence.

"Sorry...hurts," the voice said.

The light creeping through the slits of his eyelids widened as he worked his eyes open a bit more. A figure hovered over his lower body.

What had happened to him? He struggled to make his thoughts work. Buffalo... His horse had been running beside a bull. He'd drawn his arrow. Hit his mark.

The sensation of flying swept through him, then the pain searing his leg intensified.

Now he remembered. The sharp point of a rock had pierced just above his moccasin. He'd lost his horse that day, too, and had turned back toward the mountains on foot.

He glanced around him, but his eyelids wouldn't open wide enough for him to see much. Only enough to know he must be in the mountains now, what with all the rocks and trees around.

He shifted his attention back to the figure. She must be the woman he'd heard before. Then another form joined her.

A man, from the sound of his voice. White Owl should get up. He had to find out who these strangers were. Learn whether they be friend or enemy.

But he had no strength. Not even enough to keep his eyes open. His lids drifted shut, and he forced his focus on under-standing their words.

The man was speaking now. "...looks bad....cut off....leg."

Surely he didn't mean what it sounded like. Did they think him dead that they would slice off his limbs?

He worked to gather every bit of strength he had. No matter what, he would show them he was very much alive.

CHAPTER 2

*L*ola glanced up at the injured brave's face. Dark eyes stared back at her, sending a jolt through her chest. His lids were only partway open, casting shadows that made the eyes appear black as charcoal.

She swallowed. "Hello." Did he speak English? Communicating with him would be so much easier if he did. "Can you understand me?"

"Yes." Though his voice held a rasp that spoke of pain, there was a richness to it that rumbled through her.

"You understand English then. Good. Can you tell me what happened to your leg? The wound has festered badly. I have a salve, but I'm not sure it's strong enough to help what's happened here." Now she was rambling, and speaking things better left unsaid. She didn't want to take away his hope of recovery.

She pressed her mouth closed and waited for him to answer, letting her gaze take in his features while she waited. She'd never been this close to a native, at least not when she could study him so closely. The strong lines of his face, the skin darker than her own, the sharp angle of his cheekbones—they all combined to form the appearance of strength. But it was his eyes, the sooty lashes that separated just enough for her to peek into their depths. These were what drew her attention.

He was watching her too. The scrutiny itched like a woolen collar, but his expression seemed more curious than calculating. He hadn't answered her question either. If he knew only a few English words, perhaps she'd rambled too much for him to understand. Better to try once more. "How were you injured?" She pointed to the section of his calf they'd exposed. Even a glance at the fiery flesh and putrid seeping sore made her middle churn.

His gaze flicked toward the leg, and lines etched in his brow. He likely couldn't see the wound, but she could imagine how fiercely it throbbed.

"A hunt. Buffalo. Fell...on rock." The words seemed to exhaust him, for his eyelids drifted fully closed, those long lashes resting on his chiseled cheekbones.

Then they flew open just as footsteps sounded behind her. "Lola, my dear. Here's your smaller pack, and this tonic was all I could find that could be considered medicine. I don't remember adding it in to our things, so Will must have packed it."

She reached for the satchel and bottle Mr. VanBuren held out, then nodded toward the brave's face. "He's awake. And he speaks English." Some anyway.

Mr. VanBuren eyed the man with a skeptical expression. "What's his name?"

She barely kept from raising her brows. He could just as easily have asked the stranger, but maybe he thought she already had.

She turned to the Indian, and he answered without her having to pass along the question. "White Owl."

Mr. VanBuren's brows had gathered as though he was trying

to understand a phenomenon, so she responded to the brave herself. "I'm Lola Carson, and this is one of my traveling companions, Mr. Ike VanBuren. His son, Will VanBuren, is staking out our horses."

She couldn't tell if the man understood everything she said or not. His eyes roamed her face as though seeking something. She could worry about what he might be looking for later. For now, his leg needed a great deal of care.

After extracting a pair of stockings she hadn't worn in weeks from her pack, she dipped half of the garment in clean water. Now came the daunting task of cleaning away the foul liquids on White Owl's leg. "This will hurt. I'm sorry for that. I'll be as gentle as I can."

When she'd cleared the mess on the unbroken skin around the injury, she glanced at the man's face. His eyes had closed tightly, lines of pain forming around them.

She bit back another apology. She simply had to get through this so they could both rest easier, though *her* discomfort was nothing compared to his.

At last, she'd cleaned, salved, and bandaged the wound. Later, she would unfasten the cloth she'd used for a bandage and apply new salve. Would that be enough? The entire half of the leg beneath the knee had swelled as far as the skin would stretch, and the area around the wound had turned a brackish black. If a doctor were here, would he think the limb so damaged it would need to be cut off? If it came to that—if she couldn't get the wound to heal—could she do such an awful thing in order to save his life?

No. She would never be able to cut off a man's leg. To sever bone and arteries. Even if she had the proper tools. She certainly didn't know enough to staunch the blood. If she attempted such, it would be certain death for him.

Yet she might have to stand by and watch him die anyway.

She stiffened her spine. She would do everything she could for him. And maybe they could find someone else in the area who knew him, or at least better knew how to care for an injury like this one.

"The meal's ready. Come and eat, both of you." Will squatted by the fire he'd built, scooping out food from the pot—food he'd cooked himself. Those were normally her duties, and the edge in his tone told her he didn't appreciate having to take them over. Surely he didn't begrudge this injured man nursing care.

She poured the remainder of the clean water over her hands, then stood and moved to join the others by the fire.

Will patted a log beside him as he smiled at her. "I brought a seat for you."

She hesitated. More often these days, he acted as though they were courting.

But they weren't. And she had no desire for such a situation with him.

She hadn't yet summoned the nerve to tell him that, not when the three of them worked and lived in such close quarters on this journey. The awkwardness might make things very difficult.

For now, she settled on the log he motioned toward and took the bowl he offered. She would eat quickly and see what could be done to make White Owl more comfortable.

Her first bite of corn mush nearly choked her—far too thick and dry. But Will was watching, so she worked for a smile. "Thank you for cooking."

He seemed to take that as a compliment, for he nodded with a satisfied curve of his mouth and took up his spoon.

She managed to swallow a second bite, then reached for her tin cup and scooped a drink from the clean water pot. After a sip, she poured the rest into her corn mush. "This is a good meal for our patient too. Who knows how long it's been since he's eaten." Or had even a sip of water. Why hadn't she thought to offer him a drink before attending the wound?

"Think you got his leg doctored up?" Will asked the question around the bite in his mouth. Despite having attended university, his manner of eating always shocked her. Maybe it had grown worse on this journey—the farther west they traveled, the quicker he shoveled food in his mouth and the less he cared if it dribbled down his chin.

She focused on her own bowl and his question. "I've cleaned it, and I'll keep rubbing on fresh salve every few hours. The festering is bad, though. I'm not sure what I can do will be enough."

He glanced sideways at her, then returned his attention to his food. "Wonder if he'll make it after we leave."

She could only stare at the man, the sight of him making the food in her belly churn. He couldn't mean his words the way they sounded. "We'll stay here and care for him until he can manage on his own."

Will's head shot up, and his gaze roamed from her to his father, then back to her. "Why?" He must have seen the shock on her face, or maybe the thunder building inside her blazed in her eyes, for he didn't wait for her answer before hurrying on with a more appropriate question. "How long do you think that will be?"

She forced a breath out. Forced her shoulders to ease. She would answer his first question, too, for apparently he needed reminding. "He's a person just like you and me. He's hurt badly and very sick, and as far as I can tell, he has no one else to help him. Of course we'll stay and do everything we can. I don't know how long it will take. A few days, I'd guess."

Using her cup, she scooped another helping of water, then stood, bowl in one hand and cup in the other. She no longer had a desire to eat or sit near this man. White Owl needed her far more than anyone else right now.

~

*S*ome of the mist had finally cleared from his mind. White Owl listened for sounds around him before he ventured his eyes open.

A rustling whispered, like leather scraping against itself, but not quite.

He eased open an eyelid, then the other as the brightness of day increased the pounding in his head. His eyes settled on a figure and memory slipped back in.

The woman. She'd even made an appearance in his dream. How could he have forgotten her?

Either he moved or she sensed him watching, for she looked at him. She had a nice smile, one that softened her expression and brightened her eyes. "You're awake."

Before he could summon enough moisture in his mouth to answer, she shifted closer to him. "Here's some water for you. I think you went a long time without food or drink."

He tried to take the cup from her hands, but she didn't release it, only lifted the metal to his mouth. He didn't fight her for it, just raised his head to drink as she poured. His body craved the liquid too much to risk losing the chance to quench his thirst.

When he'd emptied the cup, she pulled it away. He needed to sit up, but his body still possessed so little strength. He would find enough energy soon to rise, but for now he could let himself rest while he questioned her.

And he had to do so in English. As he strained to find the right words, the pulsing in his head intensified. He could understand the language much better than he could speak it.

If only she knew how to hand talk. It would be so much easier to communicate through the signs all the tribes and many of the white trappers used. Perhaps she did. It might be worth a try.

He managed the sign for *where are you going?* Though lifting his arms made them ache.

She eyed him with her head tipped, curious confusion clouding her gaze. It seemed he'd have to find words in her language.

"Where...do you go?" There. He'd managed the right ones. Hopefully.

She nodded understanding. "We're traveling west, searching for my brother. My half-brother, that is. We've been told he might have gone over the mountains, so we're trying to reach him there before the snow makes travel too hard."

It took White Owl several heartbeats to decipher her meaning through the fog in his mind. Even then, he'd not caught everything. But *west* and *mountains* and *snow* and *travel* were clear enough. Should he tell her how the snow would already make travel through the mountains difficult? With winter already come, riding through the Lolo pass would be nearly impossible for anyone who didn't know the trail.

He looked past her for the other two men who'd been here. The older fellow sat by the fire with a rifle in his lap. The barrel was open as though he was cleaning it, but the fellow's focus hovered on White Owl. The younger man didn't seem to be here now. From the little White Owl had seen, neither of these two looked as if they'd been through a mountain winter before.

He shifted his focus back to the woman. "Snow...cold. Better go..." He struggled for a way to describe the route in her language. Then he pointed to the south. "Small mountains." He could draw a map in the dirt to better show what he meant, but that would take more work than he could manage right now.

A frown wrinkled her brow. "You mean to the south? That's a farther journey, yes? We hoped to cross the peaks before a deep snowfall comes."

The tromping of heavy feet sounded coming up the slope, and White Owl jerked his gaze that direction.

From the rhythm of the stride, it must be a man, though he made as much noise as a bear. The younger man came into view, and though his stride didn't slow, his gaze took in all three of them watching him.

He was puffing by the time he reached their camp, a weakness no decent warrior would ever show. It wasn't difficult to see the flinty look the man sent White Owl, nor the way his expression shifted as he turned to the woman. A softer look, yes, but there was still something hard in the expression.

He removed his hat and swiped his sleeve across his brow. "I found an easy pass between those two mountains. The trail looks well traveled. A good route."

Then his gaze flicked toward White Owl. "He's awake. Good. The leg healing?" Why the sudden interest in White Owl's well-being? He'd not shown concern before.

The woman—he couldn't recall her name, no matter how hard he strained—straightened, her bearing turning regal. "I was about to bring him food. The leg still looks bad though. Just as swollen and seeping." She moved to the fire, maybe getting that food she'd mentioned.

White Owl's belly gnawed, but a churning also worked through him at the thought of swallowing something. Whatever he took in may not stay, but he had to try so he could regain strength.

"I've been thinking..." This from the older man, his voice a steady calm that eased the tension in the air. "I was injured once while visiting my sister's family in a little village outside Pittsburg. The place was so remote it hadn't even a doctor, only a midwife who also advised on injuries. She rinsed my wound with saltwater. Said that would stave off festering." He directed his attention to the woman. "Have we enough salt to spare?"

"Of course. I think I've heard that too, now that you speak of it."

"Better warm the water enough for the salt to dissolve well."

But bring food first. Now that the thought of filling his belly had taken hold, his body seemed even fainter than before. Yet he wouldn't ask for anything.

Perhaps she'd heard his thoughts, for she moved back to his side and dropped to her knees. "This is meat stew. Are you strong enough to sit up?"

He would make himself strong enough. As he braced his elbows to lift himself, his own breath came in quick gasps.

When he finally sat upright, the world around him swam as the throbbing in his leg pounded louder, pulsing all the way through him. A warm cup pressed against his palm, and he tightened his fingers around it, gripping hard to stop his vision from blurring.

"Lola, perhaps he could scoot over to lean against that rock." The older man's voice again, and his words finally raised White Owl's memory. The woman was called Lola. She'd spoken another word with it when she gave her name, but perhaps that second part would come back to him later. For now, this shorter cadence seemed to fit her.

"Let's help you eat first so you can build up your strength to move." Her voice had softened so only he could hear her.

The lightness in his head settled enough for him to focus on the spoon she lifted to his mouth. He took the bit of meat and juice, chewed, then swallowed, imagining the food spreading through his body, infusing energy into every part of him. His arms grew stronger, his breaths deeper, his eyes sharper. He opened for another bite, and this time he let his gaze roam to the woman's face.

Perhaps that had been a mistake.

Her eyes caught his, locking his focus in a tight hold. Lola. He'd never met a white woman, and certainly never imagined there would be this...mystery that drew him. And beauty. She carried herself with a grace that made him barely see her lighter coloring. Her gaze dropped, and she scooped another bite. He should chew and swallow the one still in his mouth.

"Tell me, uh, White Owl." The older man spoke again. He finally deigned to address White Owl directly now, it seemed. "Are your people nearby? Were you with friends when you had the, um, hunting accident?"

White Owl flicked a glance at him. "No." That fact required no great memory to recall. He'd left all those who knew him behind. He needed a fresh start.

But if this was any sign of what the rest of the journey held...

Yet God didn't rely on signs and oracles like the sun god did, not according to the missionaries. White Owl had to reach them to learn more, to hear the rest of the words in the Book. He had to get back that connection he'd felt the night of the storm and the days after. He would find that quiet voice again. He simply had to learn how to hear it.

"No friends at all? Where do you live?" The man's voice held a tone that questioned whether White Owl spoke the truth.

He met the elder's gaze even as he accepted another bite from Lola's spoon. "I am traveling. The village I come from is far from this place."

Lines gathered across the man's face, but he held his tongue. The younger one had settled by the fire and now filled his belly with food also. Only the scraping of his metal dish sounded in the quiet that sank over them.

A good thing, for exhaustion weighed even heavier over White Owl's body than before. Even imagining the food spreading strength through his limbs no longer helped.

"I think that's enough for now. You should rest." Lola's voice jerked him back to awareness, and he forced his eyes open. Surely he hadn't nodded off while sitting upright.

She'd set the cup aside and now pressed a hand on his shoulder, then rested another on his back. She was right. Better he lay back down than reveal his weakness by falling over.

As soon as his head touched the ground, his eyelids could no longer find the strength to remain open. The brush of a warm hand across his brow was the last sensation he felt before the blackness closed in.

CHAPTER 3

"*I* think we need to look for someone." Lola tamped down the worry building in her chest as she glanced from Mr. VanBuren to Will. "I know he said his people are far away, but maybe someone will know them and can send a message. I'm sure his family would want to know of his illness." That one time White Owl had awakened and sat up to eat had given her hope, but clearly that hope had been premature. He'd not fully awakened since then, and his fever had spiked again last evening. She could see no improvement in his leg either.

She focused on Will. "Can you ride out and search today? Maybe go the opposite direction from where you went hunting yesterday. I'm worried. I think his family needs to be told."

Will's chin took on that stubborn jut. "I don't like leaving you alone with him. If he wakes up again, he could be dangerous. We don't know the man."

She didn't try to hide her frown. "We've taken away his weapons, and he's shown no sign of ill will. Besides, he's so weak he could barely sit up yesterday." She looked to Mr. VanBuren. "Even if his strength did return, surely the two of us could hold our own." Mr. VanBuren usually gave his son more credit than Lola did, but she had a feeling he would stand up for himself here.

He obliged with a vigorous nod that wiggled the skin at his jowls. "Of course we can." He turned to Will. "She's right. You should try to find someone who knows the man. With a wound like that, there's a good chance he won't survive. We should get word to his people if we can so they don't wonder what came of him."

Her belly twisted at her own fears so clearly described.

Will's mouth pulled tight as he eyed his father. "I suppose I can ride back to the plain and search a little. That seemed to be a route more heavily traveled. Once I find someone, I'll try to bring them here to retrieve him so we can be on our way."

That remained to be seen. Unless he found someone who truly knew White Owl and could get him home safely, she wouldn't be leaving the man. Not until she knew he would make a full recovery. Or if he succumbed... But she couldn't let her mind follow that path. Not unless she had to.

She gave Will a thankful smile. "I'll pack a bag of food for you to take."

He only grunted in response.

And it seemed he wasn't eager to leave, for it took him a full hour to load his pack and saddle his horse.

At last, they watched his mount pick its way down the mountain, skirting the trees. She eased out a breath, letting her tension slip away with it. For some reason, having Will around White Owl made her nerves clinch tight. Maybe the way Will looked at their new friend with such distrust, or perhaps the way he seemed to care so little about whether he lived or died.

She glanced around the camp to see what should be done next. She'd already put away the food and dishes from their morning meal. This would be a good time to wash the bandage she'd removed from White Owl's leg. At least Will had brought up plenty of fresh water from the creek.

Mr. VanBuren settled into what had become his usual seat, perched against the rock with a blanket behind him for padding. He reached for *The Pickwick Papers*, one of the three books he'd brought on the journey.

White Owl still lay painfully still, his breathing labored like it had been all night. As far as she could tell, other than the rise and fall of his chest, he hadn't moved. Lola had a friend who sat with the patients at Pennsylvania Hospital. She had once said that unconscious patients benefited from loved ones talking to them. This man hardly knew who Lola was, but perhaps simply hearing a human voice might help.

After scraping a few flakes of soap into the pot of clean water she'd left warming by the fire, she carried her work to sit beside her patient. She dropped the soiled bandage into the water and dared a look at his face. What should she say?

Asking questions would do no good, though she had aplenty. Since he wasn't awake to hear or respond—or judge, for that matter—perhaps she could simply tell him about their journey. Mr. VanBuren was close enough to hear, so she'd have to simply give facts, not her thoughts on it all.

She swished the cloth through the water to loosen the putrid crust clinging to the fabric. "I know I mentioned that we were traveling to see my half-brother, but you might be interested to know why. I've never met him, actually. I didn't know he existed until my father's passing. It seems my father had another life that began just after my birth, a life I never knew about." She did her best to keep bitterness from creeping into her voice and dared a glance at Mr. VanBuren.

He'd been her father's closest friend, like an uncle to her, and even more so since Papa's death. They'd talked at length about the revelation her father left in his will. Mr. VanBuren knew well her feelings on the matter—at least the ones she could put words to. The anger and betrayal she'd felt in learning that her father had carried on with another woman while being married to her mother. But that wasn't something she planned to tell this brave, not even while he was unconscious.

She inhaled a steadying breath and refocused on her story. "When my father died, he left our house to me and this other son, whom I never knew about. There was a stipulation that I find this brother and tell him of his inheritance within one year. If I don't have his signature on the deed, I'll be forced to leave my home." Her voice trembled as she put into words her father's awful scheme. How could he yank her shelter—her entire life— from her hands so callously?

The two of them had not always seen eye to eye. He was a businessman, certainly not affectionate like the fathers of some of the girls she'd attended school with. But he'd provided a very comfortable home for her and allowed her to pursue any hobby she wished. She'd never had an inkling he would turn against her at his death.

"I was able to track down my brother as far as the church where he'd worked. It turns out he'd become a preacher." Once more she had to work to keep bitterness from her tone. "Imagine that, an illegitimate son teaching others about how to follow the Holy Scriptures." This time she didn't glance at Mr. VanBuren, but she could feel his censure anyway.

Or perhaps that was her own conscience. Why was she digging so deep into the story now? Better to speak of the journey ahead.

"It took some doing, but we were able to track him and the group he traveled with as far as a Blackfoot Indian camp north of here." Realization slipped in, and she studied the clothing White Owl wore. Nothing particularly distinguishing, except maybe the white feathers tied in his braid. Those probably went along with his name. "Are you Blackfoot, by chance? I should have thought to ask when you were awake. Perhaps you're even from that village. Perhaps you've met my brother—Caleb Jackson is his name. He's traveling with at least two other white men and one Blackfoot Indian. We were told they went south to seek the brother of one of the white men and likely traveled on across the mountains. That's where we're going now. Two years have passed since he left that village, so we're in hopes he might have settled on the other side of the mountains. Or at least someone there will know where he's gone next." And all this she had to do within the next seven months.

It had taken five already to gather her determination and track Caleb as far as she had. That had included the time for Mr. VanBuren to send for his son so that he could accompany them. She wouldn't have trusted a stranger to travel with her, but having her father's dearest friend had given her the confidence to strike out.

She dropped her gaze to White Owl again, and her breath caught at the way his eyelids parted. He was awake? How much had he heard? Maybe his understanding of her language was slim enough that he'd not caught most of what she said.

She worked for a bright tone in her voice. "How are you feeling?"

His lips parted, an action that seemed painful.

She reached for a cup of water. "Drink this." Slipping her hand behind his head still felt too intimate with this stranger. A man. An Indian.

She did it anyway, placing the tin against his lips so he could drink until he'd had enough. When he laid back, his eyes opened farther, and she leaned away as he studied her face. That scrutiny made her chest tighten, and she fumbled for words to fill the quiet. "It's good to see you awake. I'm sorry for talking so much. I thought it might help bring you back to us." She raised her brows. "It seems to have worked. How are you feeling?" She held her face in an expression that showed she was expecting an answer, just in case he'd not understood her English well.

He parted his lips once more, and this time the act didn't appear as difficult. "Better." It seemed that was the only answer she would get. At least he'd understood the question. Then he spoke once more. "I am...Shoshone. Not Blackfoot."

Heat flared inside her, searing her cheeks and ears and seizing her throat. He'd been awake for a while and understood at least some of what she'd said. How mortifying. Had he heard those private details at the beginning? She shouldn't have spoken them aloud if she didn't want them known.

A glance at Mr. VanBuren's face showed a mixture of surprise and something like amusement. No sympathy there.

She turned back to the brave and resurrected the skeleton of her pride. "Shoshone. I remember the Blackfoot man who pointed us this direction said my brother and his friends were looking for a group of Shoshone. Have you heard of them? My brother's name is Caleb Jackson. From all accounts, he's tall and broad across the shoulders. At least two white men travel with him, maybe three, and a Blackfoot man."

White Owl studied her, but his expression was impossible to read. Maybe he was sorting through his memory to recall if he'd heard of the men. Or maybe he knew them and was trying to determine whether he should tell her.

Surely he wouldn't withhold information. She'd told him the entire story, after all. She would lose her home if she didn't find this family member whose very existence had shaken her world.

The man prepared to speak again, and she held her breath as she waited for his response. "And women."

He must not have understood what she'd said. Not a surprise since she'd rambled on far too much with her question.

She gentled her voice and took more effort to speak clearly. "Have you met or heard of three white men and a Blackfoot Indian traveling together?" She raised three fingers to accompany the word when she spoke it.

This time, White Owl's chin dipped in barely a nod before he responded. "Four white men"—he lifted four fingers—"and

Blackfoot. With women. In Nimiipuu town across the mountains."

Surprise flared through her as realization settled. He had understood. And even knew Caleb. Maybe. Assuming these were the same group her brother traveled with.

"Do you know their names? Is there a Caleb Jackson among them?"

"Yes." His eyes still regarded her, no emotion in his voice. What did he think of this situation? He surely thought her a female who spoke far too much.

It shouldn't matter what he thought. It *did* matter that he knew Caleb, though. She had to learn everything she could from him. And once he recovered... She glanced down at the leg still wrapped in the bandage. Dark puffy skin edged the cloth at both sides, showing little improvement in the swelling.

She had to get him better. Then maybe he would go with them across the mountains. Be their guide and take them directly to the half-brother she wasn't even sure she wanted to meet.

CHAPTER 4

*A*s Lola reached for a cup to scoop stew from the pot, she sent White Owl a smile. "I'm so glad you know of my brother. I look forward to hearing everything you can tell me about him. First, though, you need to eat and rebuild your strength."

She settled beside him with the dish full of meat and broth but didn't offer to help him sit up this time. The action must have been too exhausting for him the day before.

She'd only spooned two sips of broth into his mouth when he met her gaze and spoke. "Your brother has married a Nimiipuu woman. They have a boy child. They live with the others in a Nimiipuu village that can be seen from the far opening of what the white men call Lolo pass."

It took a moment for her ear to settle into the cadence of his accent, and even then, surely she hadn't heard him right. Her brother, former Reverend Caleb Jackson of Oklahoma, had married an Indian woman and now had a child with her? He'd only been gone two years. Clearly, he'd wasted no time.

White Owl had stopped speaking and was probably waiting for another bite. She obliged, once more giving him broth so she wouldn't have to wait while he chewed meat. She had a great deal to find out. "How did you meet him?" They must have been more than passing acquaintances for White Owl to have learned and remember these details.

Though his gaze had given no sign of his thoughts before, a shutter seemed to close over White Owl's eyes, shielding him even more. "He came with the others to my village. His woman was a cousin to...a friend I had." His words stumbled—maybe the English interpretation of them. Or perhaps that friend had been important to him somehow

A shadow passed over White Owl's expression, one his shield didn't quite cover.

He dropped his eyes to the cup, a clear sign he wished for another bite of stew. She gave him meat this time. She needed a moment to gather her thoughts and find the questions whose answers would help her the most.

As he chewed, she said, "So you met my brother when he came to your village. On this side of the mountains?"

He nodded.

"And have you been to the village where he is now? On the other side?"

His throat worked as he swallowed. "I know of the camp, but I have not been there with him."

She gave him another spoonful of broth. "Would you be willing to take us to the place...when you can travel again? You can ride one of our packhorses." They'd seen no sign of his mount.

A line formed between his brows, and he seemed to hesitate. "We need ride around mountains. South."

No. He'd said that before, but from what she'd heard, these Rocky Mountains extended many miles in both directions. It might take weeks extra to skirt them. Surely she could talk him out of the notion though. A bit of reasoning and a smile always worked on her father and Mr. VanBuren.

"With winter nearly on us, it seems best to take the most direct route. I'm told we can get through the Lolo pass in about a week if we push hard. How much farther would it be to take the path you speak of?"

He gave a slight shake of his head. "Snow too deep through Lolo. Go south only."

That wasn't answering her question about distance. She did her best to keep the frustration from her tone as she tried once more. "How long will it take to go the southern route?"

"Less than a moon."

A month? That would be nearly three weeks too long. They might have to take this southern trail on the way back, for the snows they'd been told of likely would have come by then. But she couldn't afford to waste so much time now if it wasn't absolutely necessary. What if Caleb had left the Nimiipuu village and they had to travel even farther to find him? She still needed to allot time to return to Pittsburg within a year, as the will stipulated.

She cleared her throat and searched for a polite way to state that they would be going directly across the mountains. But perhaps now wasn't the time to press her point. She gave him another bite of stew.

Silence settled as she focused on feeding him. He didn't look nearly as weary by the time he finished as he had the day before.

In fact, as she carried the cup and spoon to scoop clean water for rinsing, White Owl's voice sounded again. "You have the book of Creator Father's words?"

She spun to see what he meant, but he was looking at Mr. VanBuren. Or rather, the book in Mr. VanBuren's hands.

The older man's brows rose. He lifted the tome and flipped it to look at the spine, as though to see if it said *Creator Father's Words*. Then he eyed the man lying on the ground. "You mean the Bible? Have you...? You've heard of it?"

White Owl's chin dipped in that quiet nod. "Will you read it to me?"

Lola's heart stuttered. An Indian asked this?

The request appeared to have stolen Mr. VanBuren's speech also, for he took a moment to answer. "This book isn't a Bible, but I do have one with me. I would be happy to read God's words to you." He reached into his pack and pulled out his Bible, then moved closer to White Owl.

Lola kept herself busy preparing food for their other meals that day, while Mr. VanBuren's voice took up a steady cadence as he read from the book of Matthew. Her mind couldn't grasp the words, though, not when her gaze kept straying to the brave on the ground.

He'd mentioned missionaries, so perhaps he truly had been converted to Christianity. Her own conscience twinged. She'd had open access to the Bible and church services her entire life, yet she did her very best to ignore God. She'd never seen any sign He cared a wit about her. Yet this Indian so far from civilization jumped at the first chance to hear the Bible read.

Did that make him a better person than her? The thought landed hard, spreading a ripple of discomfort everywhere it touched.

~

*W*ill still hadn't returned.

The man had been gone a full day and night, and now the sun inched up toward the noon mark on the second day. The weather had turned cold, too, making their breaths cloud in the air around them.

Lola tried her hardest to conceal her worry, for Mr. VanBuren had taken up pacing during the last hour, peering down the hill every time he turned to stalk the other direction.

She'd sent enough food with Will that he'd have plenty if he needed to stay out overnight, but she hadn't really thought he would. He'd been so reticent to leave in the first place. Had he gotten lost? Or worse? Perhaps he'd met Indians who weren't quite as friendly as White Owl or the Blackfoot village they'd passed through.

Mr. VanBuren would go search for him, she had no doubt. But it seemed impossible to think one man unfamiliar with this area could rescue Will from whatever might have befallen him.

Yet if Will didn't return today, his father would have to go after him. Should she go too?

She packed away the last of the morning's food. Mr. VanBuren had already filled all their containers with fresh water, and she'd mended everything that needed mending. They had more than enough food left over for the rest of the day. She would be as restless as Mr. VanBuren if she didn't find something to occupy herself.

Her body craved a walk, but she didn't dare leave camp, not with Will missing and White Owl mostly unconscious again. Was it normal for him to remain in such a deep sleep for so long at a time? His fever came and went, sometimes soaking his clothing with sweat. Perhaps she should talk to him again like she'd done yesterday.

Except...reading would be much better. She'd proved she couldn't speak at length without sharing embarrassing details. She could read from the Bible as Mr. VanBuren had done for over an hour the day before.

Rising, she brushed the bits of grass from her skirt and turned to the older man. "Might I borrow your Bible to read to White Owl?" Or perhaps *he* needed the distraction more than she did. "Unless you'd rather do it."

He shook his head, the movement quick and jerky, just as his pacing had become. "I couldn't focus on it." Then his gaze honed in on her, anguish clouding his face. "I think I should go after him. Do you think he followed the route we came? I might find his tracks."

Her heart squeezed at the older man's suffering. Would her own father have worried this much had she gone missing in the wilderness? He'd always been so staid, their discussions almost formal. He'd never shown even a spark of emotion where she was concerned, only when their conversation turned to his most recent investment or a new venture he was researching. Mr. VanBuren had never seemed overly affectionate toward Will, but he *did* seem to care.

Should she approach him and lay a comforting hand on his arm? That felt awkward. She'd never intentionally shown that kind of physical affection to him in the past. But they'd never been in this situation before either.

She settled for an encouraging smile. "I'm sure he's on his way back. He probably went farther yesterday than he planned and couldn't return before dark. I'm glad he didn't try to find his way after nightfall. He'll ride into camp today, and maybe he'll even bring someone who knows White Owl."

Though worry lines still creased Mr. VanBuren's face, a bit of hope crept into his gaze. "I hope so. Lord God above, let it be so." He spoke those last words with his eyes drifting shut, clearly a prayer from the depths of his heart.

His eyes popped open then. "My Bible. Yes, it's in my pack. Feel free."

He returned to his pacing, hands clasped behind his back. This time his head bowed and his lips moved. Praying, she had no doubt. If it brought him comfort, good. Maybe God would listen and grant the wishes of a kind old man.

She moved toward the row of packs but hesitated as she untied Mr. VanBuren's. Did he really wish her to riffle through his belongings? His clothing? But when she lifted the flap, the stack of books lay on top. Her chest eased. After snatching the Bible, she re-fastened the ties.

A glance at White Owl showed him still in that deep sleep, the expression on his face solemn, the rise and fall of his chest steady. She could sit against the rock where Mr. VanBuren had yesterday. It was likely a more comfortable seat, but her voice didn't resonate the way his did. And part of her much preferred to settle in beside the brave. She could watch him better, be more aware if he woke.

So she took up her usual place at his shoulder, then flipped through the pages in Matthew until she found where Mr. VanBuren had left off. She'd been listening closer than she'd realized.

"'Therefore I say unto you, take no thought for your life, what ye shall eat, or what ye shall drink; nor yet for your body, what ye shall put on. Is not the life more than meat, and the body than raiment?

"'Behold the fowls of the air: for they sow not, neither do they reap, nor gather into barns; yet your heavenly Father feedeth them. Are ye not much better than they?'" So many sermons she'd heard in her life. She and her father had rarely missed a Sunday at First Presbyterian. But the words had never come to life as they did now. They'd never painted such a picture she could relate to. She'd seen so many birds on this journey, and not one had been scrawny or underfed. God provided for their needs. If only her own father would have promised as much instead of threatening to rip her home and inheritance from her if she didn't find this lost son.

"'For your heavenly Father knoweth that ye have need of all these things. But seek ye first the kingdom of God, and his righteousness; and all these things shall be added unto you.'"

What did it mean to seek the kingdom of God and his right-eousness? Righteousness, she mostly understood. Following the commandments and edicts in Scripture. But God's kingdom? Was that heaven, which came after death? Should she seek to die then?

She glanced up, and White Owl's dark eyes stared back at her. Her heart didn't jolt quite as strongly as it had the other times. She'd become accustomed to his silent attention. Finally. Those eyes had a way of seeing deeper than others did.

It wasn't as difficult to summon a cheerful smile this time. "You're awake. At last."

His gaze lifted to the sky, then swept around the camp, finally meeting hers again. "How long did I sleep?" His voice came out clearer now, more distinct.

"Nearly another day. I spooned water and broth in your mouth several times last eve, but you didn't behave as one fully awake." She'd taken the opportunity to study him, and the lines of his face had seared themselves in her mind's eye.

Even now, looking at him made her heart speed a little faster. He was handsome, no one could deny that truth. But surely her reaction came from her conscience remembering how she'd stared so.

"Is there...food?" He cleared his throat, probably to remove the rust that came from not using his voice much lately. Did he talk often when around people he knew?

She could almost imagine him standing tall and strong as he spoke with a group of other Indian men. In her imaginings, he was taller and broader than the others. Perhaps that wasn't true though. Perhaps all Shoshone men looked as he did.

Food. She gave herself an internal slap at her mental wanderings. The man lay there starving and all she could do was daydream. She'd do well to set all such notions aside anyway.

The stew from their morning meal still held enough warmth, so she retrieved it along with a biscuit she'd made the day before. "I haven't mastered baking in the Dutch oven, so the biscuits are hard. Better if you dip it in the stew."

Already, he worked to sit up, and she placed the food beside him so she could help. "Would you like to move over to the rock so you can lean against it?" He sat straighter this time, as though he had more strength now.

He shook his head, and his gaze bounced off his injured leg. The limb must hurt a great deal if he didn't want to move it yet.

A whinny sounded in the distance, and Lola jerked around to find its source. The noise had come from farther away than where their horses were corralled. Hadn't it?

She stood as Mr. VanBuren started down the slope in a hobbling run. With the scattered trees and rocks blocking her view, she couldn't see who was approaching, and she was fairly sure the older man couldn't either. She scooped up a rifle and started after him. Mr. VanBuren might have his pistol tucked in his waistband, but he likely wasn't thinking straight. Until they knew for sure this was Will—and that he came alone—they had to be cautious.

She'd nearly caught up with Mr. VanBuren when he called out. "Will!"

She could see the younger man now too. Despite his father running, Will rode toward them at a steady walk. His mouth took on a grin, as though soaking in their adoration.

When the two met, his father drew him down into a hug even before Will dismounted. The sight reminded her so much of the way she pictured the story of the prodigal son from the Bible. Her throat burned. She'd never had such a scene with her own father, prodigal or not. They'd never displayed affection, and now they'd never have the opportunity.

But when Will lifted his face to her, the roguish grin he sent her way gave the feeling he wasn't quite as repentant as the son in Jesus's parable.

CHAPTER 5

*W*hite Owl clamped his teeth against the pain in his leg as he scooted back to lean against the rock. Something about the younger man didn't seem right, and he'd feel better if he wasn't lying flat when the fellow strode up the mountainside. He needed to force himself to get up and move around anyway. Sitting upright was the first step.

Lola appeared first, climbing the last of the slope to reach the camp. When she saw him, her chin jerked up, brows raising. He'd just told her he didn't want to move to this position, and she might have realized he was avoiding the agony of dragging this damaged leg.

He would resist the pain no longer. A man faced his enemy, even if that threat was a fire raging in his limb.

She didn't comment on his actions, just moved to the flame and shifted a pot into the coals. "Will has finally returned. He went out yesterday to find someone who could get word to your people. He hasn't brought anyone with him, but I hope he met someone along the way."

The younger man—Will, Lola had called him—climbed the

rise alone. She straightened and turned to him. "We were beginning to worry about you. Where's your father?"

He could look nowhere but at Lola, and something about his smile reminded White Owl of a fox eyeing a den of rabbit young. If his own leg could have managed it, White Owl might have stood and placed himself in front of her to keep her from becoming a tasty meal.

"He's seeing to my horse. You're sure a welcome sight after riding so far. Sleeping out on the plain last night, all I could think about was whether you were safe." Now the man finally glanced toward White Owl, giving the distinct impression he'd thought White Owl had been a danger to her.

His body tensed, and if he'd been stronger, he would have charged the man. But for now, he had to hold his anger inside. This snake was more likely to cause her harm.

"All has been well here. Did you find anyone?" She motioned to one of the logs they used as seats by the fire. Then she scooped a cup into the pot and handed it to Will, juice dripping down the side. Though White Owl had just consumed his own food, the sight made his belly rumble. He wouldn't draw notice to his weakness by asking for more, though.

Will didn't answer right away, instead tipping the cup to his lips and gulping long enough to down the broth. Then he used his fingers to pick out a chunk of meat and toss it into his mouth. "I've never met a woman who could cook as good as you, Lola. Even under these...conditions." White Owl hadn't heard that last word before, but Will spoke it as though the word smelled foul.

Lola stood on the other side of the fire, hands propped at her waist as she watched the man. The smile she gave him looked far weaker than the usual light that brightened her face. "Tell me who you met while you were gone."

Will stuffed another wad of meat into his mouth and chewed a little before finally answering. "Didn't see anyone for a long time yesterday. When I reached the plain, I turned to the south because that's where he said he was from. Finally saw two Indians in the distance, but when I rode up to them, neither one spoke English. Just a bunch of gibberish. Then after I turned around in the afternoon, there was a huge war party right there on the trail. They were setting up camp too. I had to go in a wide circle around them so they wouldn't spot me. The detour took so long that I finally stopped and slept out there."

"You didn't approach them and ask if they knew White Owl?" Lola's bearing still possessed the grace she always carried, she seemed stiff. Angry.

The man paused eating long enough to stare at her. "Did you hear me say they were a war party? I'd no intention of getting scalped. There were twenty of them if there was one. You should be thankful I came back alive."

She turned away, making it impossible for White Owl to tell if she was still angry. At last, she looked back at Will, and her voice seemed to have lost some of its iron. "Did you meet anyone else?"

He shook his head as he chewed. "Just a bunch of animals. Hard to believe how much good hunting there is in this land. If I hadn't been in such a hurry to get back to you, I would've taken down a few."

Lola's hands dropped from her sides, the act hinting at despair as she turned toward White Owl. Her sharp eyes locked with his. "I'm sorry. I hoped he would find someone who could help."

White Owl didn't need that man's help, and it was time to show her so. Time to speak up. He took a moment to plan out the words in her tongue. They were coming easier now, especially since he could think clearly again. "It is well. I grow strong again. After one sleep, I will walk."

Her brows grew together, troubled lines marring her smooth skin. "I'm glad you're getting strong. The leg doesn't appear to be healing though. You're definitely not ready to walk yet."

Though what he felt in his own body rang too near her words, he had to overcome his weakness. Not just for himself. He hated that he caused the worry showing in her eyes. "One more sleep and I will be strong again."

That was a promise he made to them both.

~

The swelling had shrunk by half.

Lola stared at White Owl's injured leg. For the first time, the edges of the wound didn't hold the angry jagged lines that puffed up and oozed. She'd washed the entire area with saltwater again last night, then applied a fresh dose of salve and a clean bandage. Yet she'd done that same thing countless other times that hadn't seem to make a difference. Not a difference like this anyway.

She glanced at White Owl's face. He was watching her with an intensity that would cipher out her every reaction.

She let him see the good news in her expression. "The swelling has gone down a great deal." She turned her focus back to the leg and touched a section of unbroken skin. "It's still warm, but not burning like it had been." She sat back on her heels and released a long breath with a smile. "I think you're finally healing."

He nodded. "I will eat, then stand."

She chuckled. If he'd been able to manage this much healing, maybe he could accomplish standing too.

She tried to eat her own morning meal while White Owl inhaled his. But watching him proved much more interesting. He ate his food with gusto, his appetite and energy both much stronger than before.

Will and Mr. VanBuren sat across from her to break their

fast, and she couldn't help but compare the way Will ate to the way White Owl did. They both seemed to enjoy the fare, which should bring her pleasure. But they behaved so differently. Will stuffed in another bite while he still chewed the last, but White Owl sat with a presence that seemed almost regal.

He glanced at her, catching her staring. Though heat flamed to her face, she did her best to brush it aside. "Here's more water for you." She picked up her own cup and leaned forward to place it beside him. After returning to her food, she kept her focus on her meal.

When Mr. VanBuren dropped his plate into the wash pot, he heaved out a sigh. "I suppose I'll go move the horses to fresh grass."

She glanced at Will to see if he would volunteer to help his father. The older man was capable of managing the animals, but with six horses, the task would be easier with both of them.

But after Will swallowed down his last bite, he wiped his mouth on his sleeve. "I'll stay here and help our patient get up and around." He dropped his plate in the wash pot too, then took another swig of water. Not in a hurry at all.

"All right then." His father pushed to his feet. "Call out if you need me."

"You have your gun?" Will glanced at his father.

Mr. VanBuren tapped his waistband. "Pistol right here. Not taking a rifle as I'll need both hands for the horses."

As the sound of his steps receded down the slope, Lola finally let herself turn to check on White Owl. He'd finished eating and was watching father and son, his intense gaze likely missing nothing.

"Are you ready to stand?"

He pushed up to a sitting position, then met her look. "Yes. Little matter." He waved his hand as though shooing away a fly.

Did that mean he didn't want to make a big ordeal of it? She could understand that, though she did want to be near enough to help him if he needed it. Hopefully, Will would stay settled exactly where he sat by the fire. At the moment, that looked likely.

She busied herself cleaning the dishes. White Owl would surely be more comfortable if she wasn't staring. But she watched him from the corner of her gaze.

Keeping his injured leg out in front of him, he shifted sideways to crouch over his good foot. After hovering there for a moment, he rose to standing in a smooth motion. He must have a great deal of muscle throughout his body to move so fluidly. Once on his feet, he positioned the wounded limb a little in front of him, more of a balance than a support. Would he be able to walk on it?

A breath later, he stepped forward. One limping stride at a time, he crossed the camp. Hobbling certainly, but walking nonetheless. At the edge of the clearing, he turned, but instead of returning to his bed pallet, he met her gaze. "I go to water."

She nodded and had to fight back the urge to offer to accompany him. He clearly wanted to do this alone. And if he was going down to wash, it wouldn't be suitable for her to be there anyway.

His footsteps barely sounded as he disappeared down the slope, and in the quiet that settled in his wake, she focused more energy on her work.

Will still sat an armlength away. He'd picked up a sliver of wood to use as a toothpick, and he must be deep in thought, for he hadn't yet broken the quiet.

His words came soon though. "Now that he's recovered, we can set out tomorrow. I'd like us to make good progress through the mountains before the first snow hits."

Though she'd argued with White Owl against taking the longer route to the south—and for good reason—perhaps the rest of them should at least discuss it. The conversation might be better saved for when Mr. VanBuren could take part, but she'd rather not speak of her concern with White Owl listening, not after she'd been so insistent they needed to take the shortest trail. No need to let him know she was questioning her decision.

Better to mention it now. Though she didn't always like Will's manners, he did possess a clear way of analyzing a situation and making plans to reach a goal. "What do you think about taking a southern route around the taller mountains? White Owl says that's the only safe trail this close to winter."

His gaze jerked to her face, his surprise clear.

She shrugged. "We need to get there and back as quickly as we can, but if the Lolo trail proves impassable, we'll have to turn around and find another way."

Will didn't even hesitate, just shook his head. "We've had no snow. It's cold, sure, but that doesn't mean snow has come yet. Even if they've already had a fall or two over the higher peaks, we should still be able to get through. Leaping Deer from the Blackfoot camp said the going would be hard. We can manage it though." He seemed to realize he was talking to a woman. "If you think you can, that is. I'm sure Pa and I will be able to make the trip."

She could certainly endure anything they could. But would it be wise? "Will it be too hard on the horses? What will they eat if the grass is covered?"

He frowned. "I'm sure we can find fodder for them. Others make the journey with horses."

Perhaps he was right. But the two of them knew so little of this land. White Owl, on the other hand, had probably lived in this area his entire life.

Yet maybe he thought they weren't as capable of traveling through the challenging Lolo pass as the natives who lived in the area. For her own part, she would endure whatever she had to, push as hard as the journey required. Yet could she expect

Mr. VanBuren to do so? His advanced age would make the deprivations harder on him.

Perhaps they would need that conversation with everyone. This decision was significant enough that they should all weigh in. Even White Owl, since he'd be their guide, though she had no doubt what his opinion would be.

Mr. VanBuren returned to camp first, trudging up the slope with heavy steps. His breath was coming in huffs by the time he reached them. "Too bad we couldn't have built our fire a little farther down." He lumbered over to his usual seat by the rock. "Saw our patient by the creek. Looks like he's getting around quite well."

A bit of relief swept through her. At least White Owl hadn't collapsed yet. The water would probably refresh him, though the hike back up the mountain might be a challenge. "Should one of us go down and help him up the slope?" She had a feeling he wouldn't relish help from Will, though Will might be the most capable.

But Mr. VanBuren shook his head. "I suspect whatever that young man sets his mind to, he accomplishes. He'd probably like to do this himself."

Though the exercise might help him regain strength, she could only imagine what it would do to the swelling in his leg. At least she could see how the jaunt affected him before she agreed to set out tomorrow. Even with White Owl riding one of their packhorses, she couldn't let them leave if the journey would make his injury worse.

It felt like an hour before White Owl appeared, hobbling up the slope. His limp seemed about the same as before, though the set of his chin had hardened. He didn't look at any of them, only aimed for his bed pallet. As he lowered to the ground, every movement seemed achingly measured. He must be fighting a fierce pain.

Once he'd settled on the ground, his eyes drifted closed. She reached for his empty water cup and scooped from the clean water pot.

As she set the mug beside him again, his eyelids rose, and he looked at her. His brow glistened—not quite a full sweat, but definitely showing his exertion. Still, he dipped his chin in a slight nod. "Thank you." He didn't reach for the cup yet. Perhaps that took more energy than he had left.

Should she lift his head and help him drink? Better to let the man rest and recover on his own. But that meant they would *not* be leaving this place tomorrow morning.

CHAPTER 6

*W*hite Owl studied Lola as she picked her way up the slope. He could watch her walk for hours, with the graceful way she carried herself. Especially as the morning sunlight brightened her features.

Her gaze slid around the camp, glancing off Will, who sat by the fire carving something on a log. When her focus landed on White Owl, the soft smile that lit her eyes did strange things to his insides. She was not right for him—a white woman only passing through this area. He couldn't let his head be turned, no matter how her beauty caught his breath.

"Where is Mr. VanBuren?" Her gaze swept camp once more, hovering over the place the older man usually sat.

"He's gone for a constitutional. Following the creek, I think." Will's focus stayed honed on the wood.

The missionaries' words—or rather, what they'd read of Creator Father's words—had said White Owl was to love his enemies and pray for those who did him harm. Will hadn't quite proved himself an enemy, but he didn't seem like a friend either. White Owl was doing his best to think kind thoughts toward the man. To look for the good in him. Will had proved he possessed the ability to focus on a task for hours at a time. Watching him work had given White Owl a strong desire to see what he was making.

Lola appeared curious as well, for she stepped toward Will and peered over his shoulder. "Oh, it's lovely."

The man straightened and held up the wood, finally giving White Owl a glimpse. An animal, but from this distance and angle, he couldn't tell what kind. Perhaps a horse?

"It looks just like the buffalo we saw on the plains." Lola's voice held intense interest.

A gunshot echoed through the air, jerking them all upright as they strained to hear.

"Pa." Will scrambled to his feet, and White Owl did the same, though his injured leg still struggled to bear his weight.

Rifle in hand, Will charged down the slope. White Owl sprinted after him, ignoring the pain shooting up his leg.

He had only his knife and tomahawk, which Lola had returned to him. His bow and arrows must lie in the grassland where he'd fallen, but he still may be able to help with these.

Another gunshot rent the air.

This second sound had also been the lesser explosion from the pistol VanBuren carried. Had he found an animal that could be brought down with the smaller weapon? Or had he found danger?

What if he'd met someone on the trail? Maybe even someone White Owl knew.

The thump of Lola's footstep behind him nearly made him slow. Would she turn back if he told her to? He had a feeling this woman's stubbornness would keep her from obeying.

Better he find out the source of the excitement. Then he would know whether she would be in danger.

His injured leg buckled more than once as he maneuvered down the slope, but he stayed near trees and rocks for extra support.

Will came into view ahead, standing beside his father. The older man peered down at something on the ground. Had he killed a man?

White Owl's heart thumped harder, but he eased his speed. As he neared them, he dropped down to a walk. A hobbling walk, for his leg screamed out with every step.

Finally, a lump of fur appeared in front of the men. His tension eased out. Only hunting then. Maybe he shouldn't have assumed the worst.

Yet he didn't trust these white men.

Not that he thought they meant harm—at least, not the older one—but they seemed so foreign to this land, and they supposed anyone they met would be a danger. They had assumed *he* would be a danger.

That thought hadn't come clear until now, and though it tried to rise in anger within him, he pushed the impulse down. Lola didn't seem to fear him. At least he had one friend among them.

Mr. VanBuren looked up at White Owl as he approached. "The thing attacked me. Is it a bear?"

He took in the markings on the animal once more, then shook his head. "Smaller than bear. *Wo'ni.*" He strained to remember what one of the trappers who'd wintered with them called it. Not a wolf, but a similar word. "Wolverine."

Lola came to stand with them. "Are you hurt?"

White Owl flicked a glance at the older fellow, but the man showed no sign of damage.

He shook his head. "It charged. I just barely got my pistol drawn to shoot it before it reached me. Those teeth look like they could take out a piece of flesh."

Lola still studied the man, worry denting her brow. "We heard two shots."

Once more, VanBuren shook his head as he eyed the animal.

"He was still breathing, so I aimed once more. Didn't want him to rise up and charge again."

None of the others seemed in any hurry to prepare the carcass, so White Owl stepped forward and drew his knife. Kneeling would be a challenge, but he could endure the pain for a little while.

Both men stepped back to give him room. Did they not know how to dress what they brought down in the hunt? Surely they did, or they wouldn't have eaten before now. They were simply happy for him to do this bloody task if he was willing. *Do good to those who persecute you.* Repeating the verse was the best way to keep his frustration down.

"What are you doing?" Lola's voice stopped him just as he prepared to kneel.

He glanced at her. "Cut open. Take out meat." Maybe the men expected her to do such work. With his people, either men or women would prepare the game brought in from the hunt. But some of the tribes considered it women's work.

She shook her head. "That run down here was hard enough on your leg. You can sit, but not to work." She stepped beside him and reached for his knife. "I'll do it."

He didn't release his hold on the handle. He didn't often relinquish his weapons. But as they both gripped the tool, the side of her hand pressed against his. She'd touched him so many times these past days, tending his wound, feeding him, helping him sit up. But none of those touches had burned him the way it did now, heat spreading from the contact of their hands all the way up his arm. Their gazes locked, and hers widened, turning her usual beauty into such a stunning picture that his chest tightened.

It might have been his imagination, but her breath seemed to catch. Was that a good thing, or was she afraid of him?

She pulled her hand back, breaking the warmth of their contact. He'd not meant to refuse to give her the knife. At least, after the power of that connection, he'd not meant to deny her.

He held out the blade, handle first. She hesitated only a single heartbeat before accepting it.

But as she turned to the animal before them, reality sank in once more. He didn't want her doing this task when she'd already done so much for him. He knew well how foul his wound had been, yet she'd cleaned and wrapped it many times each day.

"No." He sounded like he'd taken leave of his senses after he'd just handed her the knife. But he shook his head. "I will pull out the meat and bring it to your fire."

"Yes, Lola. Let the man do it." Will spoke up for the first time, and something in his voice made White Owl's ire rise.

She turned on the younger man. "You do it, Will. White Owl needs to go rest his leg. I have dough to finish for biscuits. If you don't have anything pressing to do, you dress this carcass." Then her voice softened. "I'll make a stew for our evening meal, and that will go perfectly with the biscuits the way you like them."

He gave her a tight smile, though little of his heart seemed in the act. "Of course. Anything you ask."

But as Lola turned to his father, the glare Will sent White Owl nearly seared through him. *Love your enemies.*

As much as White Owl was trying to follow Creator Father's words, this man made that task far too hard.

∼

*L*ola eyed the brave riding at the front of their group. She wouldn't deny she was relieved to be on the trail again, even with all the snow they'd ridden into, but she'd have to keep a close eye on White Owl to make sure he didn't do more than his strength would allow. The last thing he needed was a setback in his healing.

The line that had formed between his brows showed he wasn't enjoying this first day out. She might not have recognized the expression when she first met the man, but so many days of watching the nuances of his thoughts on his face had helped her recognize the slight differences. She had a feeling, though, this particular look came more from the direction they traveled than from pain. Mostly.

When they'd sat around the campfire last night planning the details of their first day back on the trail, White Owl had once again made clear his opinion that they needed to take the longer southern route around the steepest mountains.

Too much snow, he'd said. *No food for horses. Too hard.* He'd been right about there being a lot of snow. After only an hour on the trail, they'd ridden into an area where the thick layers of white rose deeper than the horse's ankles, with some drifts above their knees. The animals handled it with little trouble though.

Will had argued that they could feed the horses corn mush just like they ate, if it came down to it. And the journey should only take a week or so. Surely both people and horses could stand snow and other hardships for a week.

In the end, the thought of taking a full two or three weeks longer with the trail White Owl proposed had made her decision. If she knew for sure her half-brother was still in the village where White Owl thought he was, she might not worry so much about the timeline. But what if he'd pushed farther west? She had to return with Caleb's signature on the legal documents in seven more months, or she would lose her home and her entire life as she knew it.

At least White Owl had still agreed to be their guide, even though they weren't following his advice on this first big decision.

As they traveled the snowy trail on a wide ledge around a mountain, a crack and *woosh* sounded from somewhere above.

Lola's chest clenched tight as a blanket of white rained down on the trail about thirty strides ahead. A thin layer settled on the path, but most of the snow slid on down the slope.

The first time that had happened, she and the VanBuren men had startled in their saddles, the horses jigging beneath tight reins.

A snow slide, White Owl called it.

Now, as the swish of the icy powder faded away, an unusual quiet settled over the land. Only the crunch of the horses' hooves in snow and the occasional squeak of a saddle broke the near silence.

"Are most of the snow slides small like the two we've seen?" Mr. VanBuren rode behind her, with Will bringing up the rear. The older man had begun to ask more questions from White Owl as the day progressed.

And White Owl's answers had shown deep knowledge of this land—as well as a much better understanding of the English language then she'd originally thought.

He answered now from the front, his voice rumbling loud enough to carry back to them all. "Most are. Some much bigger. When ice is heavy, then days warm, many snow slides come."

When they reached the base of that mountain, White Owl stopped them at a creek that had frozen over. The thin layer of ice broke easily, allowing the horses to guzzle while she handed the men biscuits and meat she'd packed.

Their respite didn't last long before White Owl motioned them toward the horses. It was likely easier for him to ride than stand. At least they were making good progress.

He guided them up the base of a cliff, but as the incline steepened, they veered at an angle, following another ledge that wrapped around the mountainside.

When they'd climbed nearly halfway up, a fierce crack sounded above them. She jerked and craned her neck to stare upward. The swish sounded louder than the other times, and her entire body tensed. How close was it?

A mass of white appeared overhead and the *swish* turned to a roar. Her heart seized. The snowslide was going to land directly on her.

She screamed and plunged her heels into her mare's sides. But there was nowhere to go, horses in front and behind. A sheer drop-off to her left and a cliff wall on her right.

Her entire body tensed as she prepared for the assault.

Frigid snow slammed over her, engulfing her in a frozen mass that stole her breath. *So cold.* Then silence smothered her, sealing her in darkness.

CHAPTER 7

*T*he horse beneath Lola writhed, and she fought to break free of the smothering slush. Neither of them could move more than a few inches.

Then the animal shifted forward, and Lola clawed her hands through the snow to grip her saddle. Maybe the icy crystals were loose enough that the mare could pull them both out.

But that cliff's edge...

In the silent darkness, she couldn't tell which direction was forward and which way would plunge her and Adelphia halfway down the mountain.

The mare fought harder, then surged forward. Snow clutched tight around Lola, pulling her backward. Her mount must have broken free. Lola clung to the saddle as the pressure around her grew heavier.

God, help! Her lungs burned. She couldn't breathe. Couldn't stand the weight pushing down on her.

God, is this how I'll die? She'd been a good person, but she'd also paid attention during services.

Being good wasn't enough.

She knew well she'd not given over control of her life to the

Almighty. Control had always been her friend. Yet now, she had no ability to command even her breath.

Her chest might explode any second. She could no longer survive in this icy tomb. Surely, her end drew near.

She fought to stay with the horse as it pulled her harder, smothering her with the weight of the snow on her chest. On her face.

Then everything exploded. Light struck her eyes. Air struck her mouth, and she gulped in a breath with everything in her.

Her mare struggled to free herself from the last of the snow, kicking out with her hind legs and jerking forward. Lola could only clutch tight to the saddle.

Shouts sounded around her, but she couldn't sort through whose voices called or what they said.

She could only breathe. And hold on.

At last, her mare quieted, and her own body finally took in enough breath. She closed her eyes, then reopened them, letting herself focus on her surroundings.

White Owl stood at Adelphia's head, stroking the horse as he studied Lola with a greater intensity than usual. Seeing him there, a solid support, made tears spring to her eyes. What did he see? She probably looked a fright, hunched over and clinging to the saddle, still gasping for breath, bedraggled hair soaked from the snow. She'd lost the men's hat she'd bought for this trip somewhere in the mass of white behind her. She would go without though. No hat could induce her to plunge back into that silent tomb.

The others.

She spun in the saddle and stretched up to see behind the huge pile of snow covering the trail. Both men's voices sounded, but she could only see Mr. VanBuren's hat and a bit of his horse's rump. "Are either of you hurt?"

"No." Mr. VanBuren's tone sounded a bit shaky. "Are you well, my dear? Is your horse out of the snow yet?"

Just the thought of being back in that immersive cold blackness made the trembling in her body grow worse. She forced strength into her voice. "We're out." But what needed to be done next? "I suppose we have to dig the snow off the trail so you can ride through. "

"I will dig from this side." White Owl strode around her mare's head to the snow and pulled out his hatchet.

Did she have anything that would shovel more quickly? The pot.

The others should be clearing from their side too. They would likely think of it themselves, but just in case, she called out, "Can you use something from your packs to clear snow off the trail on your end? We're working on this side."

By the time she'd pulled the pot out and joined White Owl to scoop piles of white powder over the cliff's edge, her body shivered uncontrollably. Snow had crept under her coat to dampen her clothing. She would ignore it, though. A few minutes of hard work should warm her. Hopefully, settle her nerves too.

White Owl worked without showing a hint that his injury bothered him. It certainly didn't slow his strong, sure strokes as he drove the blade deep into the snow then pushed one side of the packed crystals over the cliff's edge. Though her pot should be able to move more snow at a time, he was making a far greater difference.

At last, only a sliver of white blocked her from seeing both VanBuren men and their horses. Then White Owl's hatchet removed that final divider.

The sight of her father's dearest friend, the man who felt so much like an uncle, standing there with his horse's reins in hand brought a surge of emotion into her chest. She almost climbed the lump of snow still on the trail to give him a hug, but she stopped herself short. She wouldn't have acted that way even with her father.

Still, she let her relief and joy show in her smile. "You're safe. We're all safe."

The weight of the pot in her hands seemed to triple, and she let herself sink down onto the piled snow. "Perhaps this is a good place to rest." The VanBuren men might not even know how fully she and her horse had been buried, but her own body knew. And with every memory of being smothered, her heart surged faster until she could no longer rein her emotions back in.

The men reached for water pouches, and White Owl unfastened hers from her saddle and handed it to her. For this moment, she didn't worry so much about making sure the others didn't coddle her. Her legs wouldn't stand so she could retrieve the water herself.

After inhaling several gulps, she eased out a long breath and lowered the pouch. "Are we likely to experience more of these snow slides?" Her shivers had eased while she worked, but the cold inside her clothes caused her teeth to chatter again.

White Owl studied her, his face impossible to read. "They could be anywhere through these mountains. You are wet and cold."

She pulled her coat tighter around herself and did her best to stop the shivers.

His words captured Mr. VanBuren's notice. "Why, you're freezing, my dear. You must have gotten a great deal of snow on you during the slide."

A great deal indeed. "Adelphia and I were completely covered. Entrenched in a tomb of snow. The horse managed to pull out and dragged me with her. My clothing under my coat is soaked." The shiver that tore through her at the memory had nothing to do with her chill. She worked to keep her breathing as steady as she could manage.

Mr. VanBuren's brows dropped low, deep lines of concern marking his face. "We need to get you warm."

He was right, of course. The last thing she needed was to catch a cold. But there was no place for her to change out of her wet things and sit by a warm fire on this cliff side.

White Owl studied the slope ahead of them. "The trail will follow the side of this mountain until sun gone. Shortest way to build a fire is backtrail." He pointed the way they'd come.

Then he met her gaze, his eyes earnest though still intense, as always. "Your choice."

He'd already shown so much wisdom and hadn't resisted helping them even when they went against his advice. But she was beginning to see rather clearly how her decision might have been wrong. She'd been foolish to gainsay a man with so much more experience than she in this land.

The thought of avoiding another snow slide—of never again putting herself or any of them at risk of being buried in a silent, frozen tomb—eased some of the pressure from her chest. If they took the southern route around the mountains both going and returning, it would be at least an extra month in total.

Perhaps that was a month they would have to resign themselves to. Or something worse might happen. She couldn't put their lives in such danger.

Since Caleb had so recently been staying in the village just across the mountains, there was a good chance he would still be there. A strong likelihood they wouldn't have to search farther. That would allow plenty of time to return to Pittsburg before the deadline.

She glanced at Mr. VanBuren's worried expression, then to Will's raised brows. The younger man must have thought her look meant she was seeking his advice. "We're still willing to press on, Lola. Perhaps there will be a place on the mountain we can build a fire before tonight."

She'd been so determined to take this route, Will probably thought that still the case.

She shook her head. "White Owl is right. We should have

followed his advice earlier. I think we need to take the southern route. Hopefully, we'll find Caleb at the village where White Owl has heard him to be, and the extra month of travel won't matter."

As they turned their mounts on the narrow trail and started back down the slope, she could only hope she'd made the right decision this time. Too much depended on her getting things right.

~

*W*hite Owl stared across the low flames that illuminated the face of the man he didn't trust. Will had been speaking much through the meal, but White Owl had stopped working so hard to understand his words. He seemed intent on convincing Lola to change her mind and turn back to the trail across the Lolo pass.

Did the man care nothing for her safety? Or his own, for that matter. White Owl had seen her disappear under that mass of snow. Had felt the panic clawing his chest and throat as he jumped from his mount and pawed away at the frozen heap until he reached her own horse.

As soon as he'd freed the animal's head and front legs and had seen it didn't seem injured, he'd found a little hope that Lola might also be safe. But he hadn't rested until she'd come completely out of the snow.

Even then, the fear cloaking her face, the panicked way she gulped in air, told him just how awful being buried alive had been.

He'd learned with Watkeuse that he could never convince a stubborn woman to follow his will, but it had taken everything in him to wait until Lola made the decision to turn south on her own. Thanks be to Creator Father she'd finally agreed.

Now this fox was doing his best to change her mind and put

them all at greater risk. At least Lola seemed to be firm in her decision. Whether it be stubbornness or good sense that made her steadfast, he was thankful. *Perhaps Your hand guiding us. Thank You.*

"I don't intend to risk it, Will. Let us hear no more on the matter." Lola barked the words strongly enough that they drew White Owl out of his thoughts.

Will stared at her for a long moment, the line of his jaw tightening. He finally nodded, then stood. "As you wish. Think I'll go for a walk and get more firewood." His mouth curved into a tight smile. "Lola, would you like to join me? You might appreciate a stroll after being on horseback all day."

White Owl's body tensed. Did the man not see that she'd only just stopped shivering? She looked fragile and exhausted. A walk at night with the valley wind whipping at her was the last thing she needed.

Thankfully, she shook her head, though she gentled her voice from the harsh tone of before. "I'd rather stay by the fire where it's warm. Thank you for the offer though."

Something flashed in the man's eyes, more than just the glimmer of flame reflecting. It wasn't disappointment or resignation as a suitor might feel. It was more akin to anger, yet stronger.

That look had spoken of hatred. Simply because the woman refused to walk with him? It must be deeper. The intensity of his expression had to have come from a different reason.

As Will turned and disappeared into the darkness outside the ring of their campfire, White Owl slid a glance at Lola. It seemed his mistrust of the man had been deserving. Now he had a greater job to do—protecting this woman from one of her own people.

CHAPTER 8

"Y ou don't even want to stop in and let them know where you're going?" Lola stared at White Owl, doing her best to understand why he wouldn't want to see his friends and family when they would pass so close to his village tomorrow.

His lips pursed in a look that made her think he was regretting mentioning that detail.

But she couldn't let this go. If he thought they didn't have time for a quick visit, she had to make it plain. "We don't mind the stop." She glanced at Mr. VanBuren, who nodded his agreement. She didn't look Will's direction—his disposition had turned sour ever since she'd declined his invitation to walk last night.

She turned back to White Owl. "Please don't miss this chance on account of us."

He shook his head. "They don't look for my return yet. No need to go there." There was a sadness in his eyes that was easier to read than most of his expressions. From grief? She knew that emotion well. Perhaps he'd lost someone close to him recently, and the place reminded him too much of that person.

Her own home held too many memories of her father. Hopefully, the time away would help with that. And too, the fact that her father wasn't the man she'd thought him. She'd never imagined that the staid businessman she'd shared a home with for so many years would have kept a mistress while her mother was still alive—would have fathered a child and abandoned both the lad and his mother.

She forced those thoughts back, pulling her attention to White Owl again. He was watching her, so she caught his gaze easily. "It's your choice. If you change your mind and wish to visit your village as we pass, please know we are happy to stop. We don't have to accompany you there if you'd rather go in alone."

He dipped his chin in a nod. His mouth pulled into a slight curve, but that sadness still lingered in his eyes.

"Another good meal, Lola." Will dropped his tin into the wash pot.

She turned to him with a smile. The fare had only been warm meat and biscuits, but those were the first kind words Will had offered in a full day now.

He brushed the crumbs from his hands into the fire. "What say I help clean things up, then we can take a stroll along the creek? I saw plenty of fish when I gathered water. It's dark now, but the moon's nearly full. Who knows what we'll see."

Her chest tightened at the thought of walking with him. The last thing she wanted was to give him any hope of interest on her part. But she'd been so curt last night. Perhaps this could be a peace offering between them, and maybe she could also find a way to let him know she wouldn't welcome further advances.

She hated to deny Mr. VanBuren's hopes that the two of them would make a match. But the simple truth was, she felt no attraction to the man. Honestly, not much respect either. She couldn't marry him. Both men would have to resign themselves to that fact.

When she nodded and offered a "thank you," Will straightened, his spirits seeming to rise already. Did she really have such an effect on him? That tightening in her chest worked its way up to her throat. She had to be very careful in letting him down, what with the rest of the trip still before them.

As Will splashed through scrubbing the dishes, she packed away the food and set things to rights in the camp. White Owl slipped away to gather more firewood, and Mr. VanBuren settled on his bed pallet with his pipe.

At last she'd gathered enough fortitude to face the walk and the conversation, so she turned to Will. "Are you ready?"

He set the last plate to dry, then stood and reached out a hand to her.

She let him pull her to her feet, and his skin felt like ice around hers. "Your hands are cold from the wash water. You should take your gloves." The weather had warmed, so they'd all shed gloves and scarves.

His mouth curved into a smile. "It's nice of you to be concerned. Your hand would warm me much better than gloves though."

Now that she was on her feet, she extracted her fingers from his. His words only increased the pressure inside her. This might be her opening to speak truthfully to him, but she'd rather wait until they were out of camp and away from his father's ears. She gave him a tight smile. "You should take gloves."

She kept more than an arm's length between them as they set out. The rustle of the flowing water eased some of her tension as they walked. The moon, indeed, shone brightly, with the bank lit well enough that they could see into the water. She tucked her hands in the pockets of her coat so Will didn't attempt to hold them again.

He didn't try to speak, and that gave her time to settle in her mind how she would begin. At last, she worked up the courage to start. The noise from the water had grown louder, so she raised her voice so he wouldn't misunderstand her words. "I think there's something I should set clear between us."

She paused to take another strengthening breath, but he nudged her arm and pointed ahead. "Look. Is that a waterfall?" The sound of the river's flow had grown even louder than the relaxing rustle, but his deep voice carried over the noise.

She peered where he pointed, and the light of the round moon showed a fall of at least ten feet. "It is." Part of her wanted to grab hold of the interruption, but the rest of her wanted to force his attention back to what she'd been saying.

"What fortune. I wouldn't have thought a small stream like this had something so interesting." He lengthened his stride, and she had to do the same to catch up with him until they stopped at the base of the fall.

The water's spray shimmered in the moonlight. She'd seen a few other waterfalls along narrow rivers when she traveled with her father, but something about the simple elegance of this one settled over her like a peaceful shroud.

"Let's climb up to the top." Will's voice held a note of excitement that reminded her of an eager lad.

She'd never been one to deny a child. "All right." She started forward, and he moved ahead of her, climbing up a series of boulders that made a sort of tall staircase. She had to lift her skirt for each step, and he reached out to help her. She waved him away. "It'll be easier if I use my hands."

Irritation flashed in his gaze, but then he turned and continued upward. Perhaps he didn't like a woman who could make her own way. One more reason they weren't suited.

When she reached the uppermost rock, he already stood at the edge, staring down the falling water. He took her elbow to steady her, moving her in front of him so she could see better. There wasn't much room on this rock but enough that she could put a little space between them while still remaining on the dry part of the stone.

To hear each other, they would have to yell above the water's noise, but she had no need to speak. She could restart the earlier conversation on their way back to camp. If she were alone and the weather not so cold, she would've pulled off her stockings and sat on the edge to dangle her feet.

She leaned over to see down the length of the falls. "That's a nice swimming area at the bottom. Too bad the weather isn't warmer." The pool didn't look very deep, maybe to her waist.

A grunt sounded behind her, and she glanced back to see White Owl looming behind Will. The brave had the man by the arm, jerking him backward, nearly twisting him off the rock.

Fear widened Will's eyes as he scrambled to keep his footing.

Lola jumped sideways to get clear of his flailing legs. White Owl didn't throw him backward off the boulder, but clutched him, half dangling over its edge. The brave turned to her, and the savage look she expected to see there—a look that would accompany such actions—didn't show. Only concern. "Are you hurt?"

Her limbs trembled at the way everything had happened so fast, but she straightened to standing. "No. But he will be if he falls. Let him go." It made no sense that White Owl would attack Will, not after he'd spent the last two days helping them. He *was* helping them, wasn't he?

Had she put her trust in this man wrongly? She really knew little about him, except that his village lay just south of here and he seemed to enjoy listening to the Scriptures read for hours at a time.

White Owl shook his head, and the lines of his jaw flexed. "He was about to push you over the falls. Can you go down the rocks yourself?" He nodded down the boulder steps they'd climbed.

Push her? Will? Why in the world would he?

Those questions could be asked soon, but first they had to get off this rock.

Will started to bluster a denial, but a shake from White Owl silenced him.

She looked back to the brave. "Will you bring him down right after me? You won't hurt him?"

"I will bring him down. Ask him why he wishes you hurt."

Will's eyes rounded. "I don't. Lola, I would never. I was —" His words cut short.

They had to get off these rocks and sort this out. As much as it seemed impossible Will would hurt her, she couldn't make herself believe that White Owl would turn against them. Though it seemed he was only turning against Will.

She started down the steps, scrambling as quickly as she dared in the dark. This whole situation must be a misunderstanding. White Owl had thought he'd seen something different than what Will actually meant. It made sense that Will would have reached out to keep her from falling. She'd been leaning over the edge of the falls, though she'd been far enough back she'd not been in danger.

When she reached grass again, she stepped out of the way until the two men stood before her, White Owl still gripping Will's arm.

She nodded to his hand. "You may release him."

White Owl dropped his hold, but the tension grew thicker in the air around them.

Will shook his arm and straightened. "I was reaching out to keep you from falling. I don't know what this Indian thought he saw, but I would never hurt you." Will's voice turned gentle, his eyes pleading. "You know that, right? I would never hurt you."

He took a small step toward her, but she raised a hand to stop him. The last thing she wanted was an advance.

Turning to White Owl, she kept her voice steady. "Why were you up there? And what exactly did you think you saw?"

He seemed to work to unclench his jaw. "Coming back with wood." He motioned up the falls. "Saw you both, you moving to rock edge. He raised his hands and held them behind you." White Owl lifted his own arms, palms forward in a motion that would make it easy to push something.

His gaze narrowed. "Stayed like that too long, like making a choice. I have seen him look at you with too much anger. I do not trust this man."

A weight pressed on her chest, so much harder than when she'd worried about Will's hopes for an attachment between them. Could there be merit in what White Owl said? Surely not. He didn't know Will. He'd probably read far too much into the man's disgruntlement today.

And she needed these men to get along. Having White Owl to guide them had been a wonderful boon. She couldn't risk losing him. She also couldn't risk a breach with the VanBuren men.

She inhaled a long breath, then released it as she looked from one to the other. "I think this has been a misunderstanding. I'm sure Will meant me no harm." She tried to summon a smile for him. Then she turned to White Owl. "I appreciate you watching out for me. You don't have to worry quite so much, though."

Neither man looked reassured by her words. White Owl's jaw had clamped shut again, and Will's lips pinched in a thin line. He looked as if he had only a fingertip grip on his anger. Understandable, given what he just been accused of.

She had to get both men back to camp where they could calm and things could return to normal.

CHAPTER 9

*A*s White Owl lay under his fur covering, the rustle of bedding sounded on the other side of the fire. He cracked his eyelids just enough to see Lola sit upright, then slide from her blankets and stand. The older man's snores covered most of the noise she made. Will's breathing wasn't as loud as his father's but strong enough to easily know when the man slept.

White Owl shifted his head so he could watch Lola as she pulled her coat tighter around herself, then turned toward the creek. She strolled upriver, and with few trees and a bright moon, he could see her clearly. She didn't seem in a hurry. Hopefully she was giving more thought to what that fox had attempted by the waterfall.

Could she not see the hatred that sometimes flashed through his eyes? If she'd known the man a long time, perhaps she'd become blind to what she didn't expect to see.

And why *would* she expect such a thing? What would cause any man to despise Lola, especially to the point he would harm her? She certainly possessed a strong will, and White Owl had seen too many times how that could turn a situation bad for a woman.

He had to be even more watchful. He couldn't allow Will a chance alone with her.

If White Owl told her everything he'd seen and suspected, would it change her opinion of the man? Maybe she would at least begin watching more closely. If she wasn't by herself with him, that would make White Owl's job easier.

She'd moved far enough away from camp that they could speak quietly without waking these men. This might be his only chance to talk plainly with her.

He slipped out of his bedding and stood, checking to make sure his knife hung from the strap around his neck as he tucked his tomahawk at his waist. In this country, a wise man carried weapons even when walking to the creek. The bears should be sleeping through the winter by now, but too many other predators might be lurking around.

He padded out of camp and stayed close to the water as he walked toward Lola. From this angle, she should see him coming easily. The last thing he wanted was to scare her.

She noticed him right away and paused to wait as he approached. When he reached her side, she spoke first. "I couldn't sleep. The murmur of this current is so soothing. I thought this might settle my mind."

He stared out at the water where she was looking. The creek ran clear, about as deep as his arm and with enough rocks to keep its flow swift. Perfect for a relaxing sound.

"I have always liked flowing water too. It makes me think more. Not less." He slid a look to catch her expression.

Her mouth curved in the sweetest smile, gentle, as she stared at the water. "You're right. It's not accomplishing my purpose very well." She was silent for a long moment, then the air seemed to slide out of her. "Do you really think Will was trying to hurt me?" She turned to him, and the moonlight glimmered off her dark, searching eyes.

He wanted to say no. To take away the concern he'd brought on. But this was no time to cease worrying. She needed to be aware. "I have seen him look at you after you turn away. There is a hatred in his eyes I cannot understand. When I stood behind him on the rock, I saw him hesitate like a man coming to a decision. One that would change things."

"But why? I can't think of a reason why he would hate me. I thought he wanted to court me. That's certainly what his actions have shown, and Mr. VanBuren has spoken of the possibility more than once."

The idea of that man having Lola pressed in White Owl's chest. At the same time, his hands itched to reach out and soothe the worry from her eyes.

"Do you think Mr. VanBuren is pushing Will toward an attachment with me, and he resents it? Would that cause him to want to hurt me?"

The vulnerability in her voice was too much to resist. Especially when a breeze whipped hair across her face. He reached up and used the tips of his fingers to brush the strands back, tucking them behind her ear as he'd seen her do so many times.

Yet the contact seared through his fingers. She inhaled, then her breathing seemed to stop.

His own chest couldn't push air past the knot in his throat. He'd been drawn to this woman since the first moment he'd awakened and seen her bent over him. No, before that. The first time he'd heard the gentle rhythm of her voice while he'd been too weary from fever to open his eyes.

That voice spoke to him now. "White Owl." Though barely more than a whisper, it seemed to call him, to pull him closer.

His hand slipped behind her neck, brushing the soft hair there. Her eyelids lowered, and her face rose to his. The wisp of her breath warmed him just before he met her lips with his own.

The sweetness there was far more than he'd expected. He'd seen a man kiss a woman, had seen his own brother Yagaiki kiss his wife with a fervor that made White Owl turn away. Yet he'd never imagined such a contact could bring pleasure like this. Could connect him so thoroughly with this woman.

He wrapped his free hand around her back, and she came to him. The way she deepened the kiss ignited fire through him. Had she ever kissed a man before? So much he didn't know about her. Yet he wanted to. He wanted to know everything.

One thing he did know—he was quickly losing himself. With the last bit of his strength, he eased back enough to allow space between them. He couldn't catch his breath, and she seemed to suffer the same.

She cupped his face with her hands. Her touch was strong. Soft, but not weak. Just like the woman herself.

As he stared into her eyes, the acceptance there nearly made his knees buckle. Her lips curved in the flash of a beautiful grin. A look his own heart returned with far too much ease.

She was the last woman he should allow himself to grow close to. But he might already be too far gone to stop.

~

*W*hen she'd first awakened that morning, Lola had fought the urge to give in to shyness and avoid White Owl. After all, she'd *kissed* the man. She'd never kissed any man before—not like that, anyway—yet here she'd kissed a Shoshone brave, of all people.

She couldn't see White Owl as different anymore, not in that way. He certainly seemed different from Will—kinder, more considerate. And he had surprisingly better table manners, though White Owl appeared uneasy using a spoon.

The way he protected her, made her feel safe and cared for—she'd never felt so safe. Not really.

Yet after she'd given herself so fully to that kiss, she'd decided to retreat today. But then she'd seen him in the early morning mist, walking back along the creek, at almost the same spot their tête-à-tête had been the night before. His gaze had found her where she knelt beside the campfire. Her own lips had matched the smile he sent. Her heart definitely wouldn't allow her to back away.

So now her goal was to get to know this brave better. Nothing more. And since they were riding through a wide valley, she should move forward and ride beside him, though she would miss watching those broad shoulders and the easy way he rode.

When she pushed her mare alongside him, he slid her a look. One of those where the corners of his mouth tipped upward in a smile that seemed only for her.

As the horses settled into an even stride, she searched for a way to begin the conversation. "How far are we from your village now? Have we passed the turnoff?" She'd planned to offer him another opportunity to visit his home, but she might have already missed that chance.

He lifted a finger to point to the place where two mountains ahead of them came together. "Through that pass, we would see the valley of their winter camp."

It sounded as though he still didn't plan a visit. "And which way do you want to ride?"

He raised his arm again, this time pointing to a pass on the right side of the mountain ahead. "This will take us the better way to find your brother."

She looked at him, searching for some sign of why he resisted. His expression was hard to decipher. "Would you tell me why you don't wish to go home, even for a short visit?"

Was it a woman? The thought pressed an ache in her chest.

But that could well be the answer. A strong, desirable warrior like him must have a string of admirers eager for his attention. Perhaps even a special one. The ache twisted into a sharp pain.

Lines formed at the edges of his eyes, and as he glanced her way, sadness shone there. Then he focused forward again. "My brother has long been my only family. Our parents and a sister died when we were young. Yagaiki and I kept our lodge, hunted and cooked and grew together. Then he married and built a new lodge. His wife was kind. His daughter, I love as my own." He pressed a fist to his chest in the region of his heart.

But something in his tone foretold the next part would be sad, even sadder than two young boys forced to raise themselves after losing everyone dear to them.

"Last winter, trappers came, and when they left, the spotting sickness stayed among us. Yagaiki and Kimana both died. Their daughter, Pop-pank, was given to another. A woman who knew them all and loved them. She is a mother to my brother's child. For a time, I thought I..." His voice faltered just enough for her to realize what he must not be saying. "But she is married now, and I must give them time to grow together. My presence does not help Pop-pank stop her grieving."

The pain had only tightened in Lola's chest. He'd lost his brother, the one who had been his best friend, maybe his only friend, for so many years. And when he might have found solace caring for his niece, even that had been stripped away. If the VanBurens hadn't been riding behind them, she would've reached out to connect with White Owl, to somehow show him she felt his grief. That she wanted to make it better in any way she could. Yet she couldn't.

He spoke again, though he kept his focus forward. "Two missionaries came to our village during the summer moons—a brother and sister. They told us of Creator Father, and I have learned to trust Him. They asked if I would go with them and translate their words into the language of the people. I could not go with them at first. But later, I left to search for them. That is where I was going when you found me." This time when he slid a glance her way, his lips pressed in amusement.

The light expression in his eyes eased some of the weight pressing on her. She worked for a playful tone. "And it's a good thing we did. I thought for a while there I might have to cut off your leg just to save your life."

A snort slipped from White Owl, a very unexpected sound from this staid brave. How many other surprises would he reveal?

◈

*W*hite Owl couldn't remember a time when he'd felt as much hope as he had these last two days. Not that he expected happiness to come from another person, but the more he learned of Lola, the more he enjoyed simply being with her. Even if that only meant sitting across the fire from her as the group ate.

He still watched Will, but at least Lola hadn't allowed herself to be alone with the man. It was hard to tell if he suspected anything growing between Lola and White Owl. The confrontation at the waterfall was enough to explain the glares he sent White Owl.

Will still appeared to be trying to win Lola's favor. Like just now, when he'd offered to cook the evening meal while she enjoyed some time at the river beside their camp.

White Owl had already begun picking up logs for the fire to keep the blaze burning into the night when he heard Will make her the offer. At least it would get Lola away from him. And she certainly deserved a few minutes to herself. As much as White Owl would have loved time alone with her, he had intentionally turned the opposite direction as he picked up logs in the cluster of trees up the slope.

The older VanBuren man was settling the horses, fastening hobbles and rubbing down sweat-matted hair.

White Owl carried each armload he gathered back to drop them in a pile beside where Will worked over the fire. The man never looked up at him, but that suited fine.

Love your enemies. He hadn't intended for Will to become an enemy, but the man's own actions had made him so. And the thought of loving him settled like bad meat in White Owl's belly.

He had to make himself follow the Creator Father's wishes. But what would accomplish that?

No idea came to him as he scooped up another arm load of logs. When he started back toward the campfire, Will's quick movement caught his gaze.

The man darted a glance over his shoulder toward where Lola had gone down to the river's edge. She couldn't be seen from camp, but was Will trying to watch her anyway? Now he turned back to the food preparations and worked intently over them.

Too intently.

A tingle slid up White Owl's neck as he stepped forward quietly, like he would during a hunt. Will had the plates out that they ate from and was cutting something into one of them.

A branch snapped somewhere in the trees above, and the man jerked his head up. He saw White Owl then, and the glimpse of fear in his eyes couldn't be missed.

CHAPTER 10

hite Owl stared at Will as the man jerked his focus back to the food and scooped a cup full of stew out of the pot, then poured it into the plate he'd been cutting something into.

White Owl had nearly reached camp now, and Will scooped another cup of soup, then poured it in the next plate. "Food's ready." His voice was gruff, with no sound of the nervousness that seemed to tighten his body.

After dropping the logs in the pile with the others, White Owl straightened and glanced around. VanBuren was walking toward them from the horses, and Lola approached from the river. If Will had done something different with one of the plates, it would be interesting to see who he gave that one to.

White Owl lingered by his pack until the others sat, then moved forward and took a place between Lola and the elder. Will handed one of the untainted plates to his father and another to White Owl, as though moving in a circle as he handed out the food.

The one he'd been cutting something into he held out to Lola.

A knot clinched in White Owl's belly. What had Will put in that dish before scooping food into it? Nothing good. Every part of him tightened with conviction.

Lola raised a spoonful of the stew partway to her mouth, then held it there as she breathed in the scent. "This smells good, Will. Thank you for cooking it."

White Owl reached out and gripped her hand. He couldn't let her eat any of it.

She turned to him, her eyes widening.

"What are you doing? Unhand her." Will's voice rose like a mosquito buzzing around them.

Lola lowered her arm to her lap, pouring the spoonful back into her plate. White Owl shifted his grip to rest more gently on her arm.

She searched his gaze. "What is it?"

Maybe the way he'd reacted so strongly by the falls had made things hard on her. And since Will hadn't actually touched her that time, there hadn't been a way to prove what the man intended. White Owl wouldn't give him a chance to truly hurt her now either, but perhaps he could allow this situation to go a bit further to catch Will more securely in his wrongdoing.

He pulled back his hand and took his own plate, then held it out to Lola. "Take mine. I will eat yours." With his eyes, he tried to let her know how important it was that she follow along. Watkeuse never would have obeyed such a command, but maybe Lola would trust him. Maybe.

With the faintest of nods, she took his dish and handed hers to him.

A glance at Will showed a smirk on his face, as though he was satisfied with the way things were progressing. Perhaps both bowls of food were tainted. Or none. There was one sure way to find out.

He lifted the plate and turned to the elder VanBuren. "You did not get as much. Take some." Before either man could stop him, White Owl dumped half the stew from the plate in his hand into Mr. VanBuren's.

"What in—" VanBuren jerked back, spilling some of the food out of his dish. Red swarmed his face and he slammed the plate on the ground.

He leveled a glare on White Owl first, then turned it on Will and even glanced at Lola. "I want to know what's going on here. And I want this foolishness to stop." He turned to White Owl. "What's the problem with the stew?"

This felt too much like being called out by his older brother, but White Owl did his best to keep hold of his temper. He'd not been in the wrong here, but letting words fly loose would make it appear so. "I saw him put something in the plate he gave her. I wanted to test whether he meant good or harm."

The man studied him for a long moment, then seemed to decide White Owl spoke truth. He turned to his son. "What did you put in there?"

Will straightened, his scowl turning self-righteous. "I found some berries I thought would add a bit of flavor. There weren't enough for everyone, so I gave them to Lola."

The story sounded like one that could be true—with another man. But Will's other actions... It was too hard to believe he would do this only for Lola's pleasure.

White Owl eyed the man. "Why did you do it in secret? Why did you look behind you to make sure none saw?"

Will shrugged then raised a brow. "I didn't want the rest of you to know what you were missing. I was trying to be nice." But nothing about the twist of his mouth appeared nice.

Still, White Owl held his tongue.

"Where did you find these berries?" Lola spoke for the first time since she nearly ate the tainted stew. She studied Will with a look far too calm. Did she think White Owl imagined the danger this time also?

The pale-haired scoundrel glanced behind him toward the

river. "Down by the water. I picked all that were there." The smile he turned on her made it hard for White Owl to tamp down his anger.

Love your enemies. If he repeated the words in his mind, maybe he could contain himself.

"That was nice of you to think of me. What did the berries look like?" Did she really believe he'd done it from kindness? Her voice and expression were so serene. Was she trying to keep him calm? Surely she had a deeper reason for acting so. The Lola he was coming to know had too much sense to be blinded by this man's thin charm.

"Red and round. Small, like this." The man held his fingers no farther apart than the width of a piece of bark.

She turned to the elder VanBuren and held out her hand. "May I hold the plate? I'd like to taste one."

White Owl's entire body tensed. Had she lost her senses? The food was poisoned, he had no doubt.

As she received the dish from VanBuren, she slid a sideways glance to White Owl. The look seemed to say, *Wait. Trust me.*

The same look he'd given her when he'd asked her to trade plates. And she *had* trusted him.

Could he do the same now? Though it warred against every one of his instincts, he kept himself still.

She took up the spoon and stirred the stew, then scooped some and lifted the bite. She eyed the liquid inside. "I see the berry. It does look tasty."

Then she turned to Will and poured the contents of the spoon into his dish. "You try one too. We should all get the pleasure."

It took everything in White Owl not to grin at her cunning. Will dropped his plate to the ground. "I'm not hungry anymore." He stood and nearly stomped to the horses. "I'm going for a ride."

As he jerked up his horse's rope, the animal threw its head

back in surprise. Will sprung aboard, then yanked his horse toward the river and dug in his heels.

~

"*I* know you're right, but I don't know what to do about it." Lola kept her voice low as she knelt beside White Owl at the river's edge to clean the dishes.

After Will had galloped away on his horse, the air in the camp had been thick with tension. White Owl had told them what he saw Will do as he prepared food. Mr. VanBuren had protested that Will must not have meant harm, but his defense seemed feeble. As though he wasn't sure his words were true.

She'd pulled out cold meat and biscuits—the same thing they'd had for lunch on the trail. None of them had eaten very much. Then while she gathered dishes to wash, Mr. VanBuren pulled out his Bible and settled on his bedroll. He'd not offered to read aloud as he often did. Maybe he would find answers in those pages. She almost wished she had something like that to turn to.

For now, she was hoping White Owl would have insight for her.

"How long have you known him?" He reached for another of the plates soaking in the calm water at the edge of the river, then scrubbed its surface with sand. She'd never have expected that a Shoshone warrior would be cleaning dishes at her side. But when she'd gathered the tins and started to the river, he followed, taking the load from her arms and matching her stride.

"I've known his father all my life. Mr. VanBuren and my papa were close friends as far back as I can remember. Will lived at boarding schools mostly. His mother died when he was young, like mine, and I think his father thought that a better situation than hiring a tutor. So I only saw Will a few times until we set out on this trip."

She took a clean plate from him, rinsed it once more, and added it to the stack. "When I realized I would need to travel west to find my half-brother, I asked Mr. VanBuren if he would accompany me. He wanted Will to come, too, so we'd have a younger man for the harder tasks. That made sense, and I've always thought the distance between father and son was sad. It seemed good to give them time together." If only she'd known what challenges Will's presence would bring.

They worked in quiet for several minutes. White Owl seemed to prefer silence when he was thinking through an answer. And she loved the way the lack of words made other connections stronger, like working in tandem to clean the dishes. This felt right, being at his side. Talking through problems together.

At last, White Owl broke his silence. "Creator Father's words say to love my enemies and pray for those who hurt me." He slid a look at her, his expression sober. "I think he means to pray for those who hurt you too. But that is the hardest part for me. I have reminded myself of this command many times with this man."

A tightness clogged her throat. She'd wondered often what restrained White Owl when it looked like he wanted to retaliate against Will. She'd never thought it was the Scriptures that held him back. What a good man he was.

A far better person than she. She should not let him attach himself to her, should push him toward someone better. If only she knew such a person in this area. Perhaps the missionary woman he'd spoken of, the sister traveling with her brother.

The thought burned her throat, clearing away the knot but still making it impossible to speak without a hitch in her voice. "After you take us to Caleb, will you keep searching for the missionaries you were going to find before?"

His gaze roamed her face. Had he heard the pain she tried to conceal from her tone? "I had planned to."

Did that mean he'd changed his mind? She had to know for sure, had to know what he was thinking. "Will you still?

His brows drew together as he studied her. "I don't know."

She could barely breathe with the weight on her chest, but she managed two more words. "You should."

A shadow dimmed his eyes, something like pain. But he turned back and reached for the last dish.

She didn't want to hurt him, but more than that, she wanted the best for him. Even if that wasn't her.

As she waited for him to hand her the plate, silence settled again. But then White Owl spoke. "Do you trust VanBuren?"

Was he shaking off her words? Her suggestion that he not attach himself to her? Perhaps he simply needed time to think and accept them.

She thought through the answer to his question. She'd always loved Mr. VanBuren. And yes, she'd always trusted him. She couldn't say for sure how she felt now. Everything seemed such a muddle. But she could say what she knew to be true. "I always have."

White Owl gave a nod, though he kept his focus on the sand filtering through his fingers. "Maybe you should talk to him. He will know his son best, even though they have been apart."

Maybe. It had turned out she'd not known her own father at all, though she'd lived with him her entire life.

But White Owl's words seemed wise. They felt right as she weighed them.

"All right. I'll speak with him now, before Will comes back."

CHAPTER 11

$\mathcal{M}$r. VanBuren had been asleep when Lola and White Owl carried the clean dishes back to camp. The man must surely be worn out from the long days in the saddle, and she didn't have the heart to wake him.

Now another day had passed, and there hadn't been a spare moment when she could pull him aside without raising questions in Will. With dusk coming, they would be making camp soon. Surely she could find a chance to speak with the older man during the evening.

Maybe she could even ask him to take a stroll with her. That might spark curiosity, since she'd not suggested such before on their journey. But that would simply have to be. The heaviness in the air among them was so thick it nearly smothered her. Did the older man know what Will was thinking? Or was he as worried about his son as she was?

The meal was a quiet affair, and she only wished she could blame the solemn faces on her poor cooking skills. Will neither spoke nor looked at any of them unless asked a direct question.

Sadness hovered over Mr. VanBuren, and the pain in his eyes was too hard to look at.

She had to make the situation right.

They weren't camped near flowing water this time, but Will had hiked up the slope to fill her pots from a tiny spring. As she was cleaning the used tins, Mr. VanBuren pushed to his feet. "I'm going for a walk to get some air. I'll bring back a load of firewood."

Her heart leapt. "Wait. I'll come with you." She dropped the half-cleaned plate back in the water and shook the drops from her hands.

He waved a staying hand in her direction, though he didn't stop walking away. "I'll just be gone a few minutes. No need for a chaperone."

The words stung, probably more than he'd meant them to. She could have said she had something she wanted to discuss with him, and he might have allowed her to come. But he clearly didn't want her along. More than anything, she needed a father's guidance, but she should have known better than to expect that from a man who wasn't even a blood relative.

She turned back to her work, focusing on the dishes so her emotions didn't show on her face. Will had settled back with his carving, and White Owl was sharpening his knife. She could feel his gaze on her though. He might suspect her disappointment, but she wasn't ready even for him to see how deep it ran.

By the time Mr. VanBuren returned, she had been working to find things to keep herself busy. She'd even gone to check the horses and feed them scraps from the meal. She didn't dare linger there long though, for that meant Will and White Owl were alone together in the ring of light from the campfire. Not that she worried about White Owl, for he'd proved he wouldn't retaliate against an insult if Will launched one at him.

But Will... She had no notion what to think where he was concerned. The last thing they needed was another confrontation.

As the older man shuffled into camp, his gaze found Lola. He paused and waved her up. "I think I would like you to walk with me, my dear, if you've still a mind for it."

She sprang to her feet. "Of course." As she followed him, she glanced at the other men. They would have to manage without her for a short time. When her focus landed on White Owl, her worry eased. The encouragement shining in his eyes infused her with strength for the coming conversation.

She took long strides to catch up with the older man, though Mr. VanBuren hunched more than usual. Will's suspicious behavior must be hard on him, especially layered on top of the strenuous journey.

When she reached his side, she slipped her hand in the crook of his arm. Not something she usually did, but he seemed to need fortifying. The moonlight revealed his soft smile as he patted her hand and straightened a little.

He didn't speak, most likely waiting until they passed out of hearing distance from the camp. She could make light conversation, but both her mind and her spirit weighed too heavy to find meaningless words.

At last, he halted and turned to her, the movement dropping her hand from his arm. "I assume you wished to talk with me about Will." Shadows from the moonlight deepened the lines on his face, illuminating the sorrow that must plague him. "I wasn't ready to speak of it earlier. I'm sorry. But it's not fair to you to ignore your concerns. You may ask what you need to, and I'll do my best to answer. Truthfully."

That last word hung in the air between them. He knew how much her father's dishonesty—his concealment of Caleb—had hurt her. Truthfulness was one of the gifts she now valued most.

Her throat burned, but she gathered the questions she needed to ask. "Can you think of a reason why Will would wish to hurt me?"

Mr. VanBuren sucked in a breath and pulled back, almost as

though she'd slapped him. Perhaps she should have started with a more benign query. But this one rose above all others, and its answer might make anything else she could ask unnecessary.

He stilled, his brows gathering in thought. He'd promised honesty, and she could only pray he would carry through with that commitment.

At last he spoke. "I can't think he would. I know the two of you have never spent much time around each other before this trip. That always saddened me, but I felt I had placed him in the best position I could—the best schools. I told myself I didn't want to distract him from his studies by bringing him home very often, but I can admit now that I was afraid to be his father." His voice rasped with the same sadness that pressed through her.

"It wasn't until your papa passed that I owned up to the fact that neither of us were quite the parents we should have been. I sent Will a message and begged him to come for a visit. With so many responsibilities to tie up your father's affairs, I wasn't able to leave to go to him." He gave her a sad smile. "I also felt I needed to be there for you. I treasured our talks, the way you opened up to me, though I'm still exceedingly sorry for the things that brought you pain."

She nodded to acknowledge his words, but the last thing she wanted was to drag up the emotions that always swarmed when they discussed her father. "Did Will come to visit when you asked? I don't remember you mentioning it."

He shook his head. "When I asked him to come for a visit, he was just establishing himself as an assistant to the solicitors at Crosby and Shelton. He didn't feel he could leave at the time."

"How was he able to come on this journey then?"

.   .   .

*O*nce more, Mr. VanBuren's mouth pressed in a sad smile. "On the day he received my note about our trip, his employment there ended unexpectedly. He says they lost one of their largest accounts and no longer needed his services."

Will had been released from his employer? She hadn't known that. In truth, she hadn't really stopped to think about why he would be able to leave his home and work for so long. She'd been so caught up in her own grief and bitterness, she'd not thought much of Will at all.

"Is there anything the two of you have discussed about me that might have angered him?" Mr. VanBuren might think she was asking about an attachment with her. And perhaps she was, but also more than that.

Mr. VanBuren released a long breath. "I've spoken to him many times in recent years about how lovely you've become and how much a connection between the two of you would please me. When we were preparing to leave, I told him this would be an excellent time to know you better, and even court you if you seemed willing." He cleared his throat, a nervous sound. "I'm sorry if that's presumptuous. I feel like an uncle to you myself. I would never let him show attentions you didn't wish to receive."

She locked her gaze with his. Though she really didn't wish to discuss this topic now, she couldn't miss the chance to set him straight. "I have no intention of marrying anytime soon. And I don't think Will is the right man for me. I'm sorry if that brings pain, but that's truly how I feel." She tried to soften her tone. "But setting that aside...how did he respond when you told him that you'd like him to court me? Did you sense any anger?"

"Anger, no. He was quiet. Thoughtful. It seemed he might really be considering pursuing you. Since then, I've seen him go out of his way to be courteous to you. I admit his behavior last evening was unsettling. But I can't think of any reason he might want to harm you. It seems more believable that he truly did find berries he thought would be a special gift for you, and when he was called out, his anger stemmed from embarrassment."

Another sigh slipped from him. "His manners certainly aren't as civilized as I would have expected after all these years at the elite schools he attended. It seems he's learned more from the lads around him than from his teachers."

The knot in her belly tightened. Mr. VanBuren had no helpful insight to offer. And it seemed he didn't believe his son intended harm. Perhaps a seed of suspicion had been planted. Hopefully he would be watchful and would take notice if anything else happened. Maybe she could ensure that by asking him to.

"Thank you for answering my questions. If the opportunity arises, would you ask Will questions that might show us what he truly thinks about me? I don't mean romantically. If there's something I've done to offend him, I want to know so I can correct it."

"If the opportunity arises, I certainly will."

She exhaled her own long breath. "I suppose we should get back. I'm sure we're all ready to retire."

As they strolled the distance to camp, a deeper weariness weighted her body. Aside from clearing the air between herself and one of her dearest friends, this conversation hadn't helped at all.

She'd simply have to be watchful toward Will. And having White Owl to help keep an eye on the man eased her fears some. But that would only last another two weeks or so, until they reached Caleb's village and hopefully met him there.

Then she would have to say goodbye to the man who'd so quickly won a place in her heart. And she'd be on her own with one she no longer trusted.

～

*T*hey'd experienced remarkably good weather these past few sleeps, but the thick clouds hanging low in the sky showed that would soon end. White Owl struggled to remember any rock overhang or cave in the landscape ahead where they might take refuge from the coming rain.

Trees might be their only shelter, and if they stretched pelts between several of them, they could keep themselves and their supplies mostly dry. Wet leathers were never pleasant, and now that he'd removed the bandage from his wound, the drenched buckskin might rub the new skin raw. But being soaked in all the layers of material Lola wore might be just as miserable. They may as well stop in the cluster of woods just ahead so they could hang as many coverings as possible before the rain came.

As they reached the trees, he reined in his mount.

"Are we resting the horses?" Lola stopped beside him, and the two men halted behind her.

He slid from his saddle. "Rain comes. We should make shelter."

In the distance, a sliver of light shot through the sky. A breath later, a rumble crept through the air. His body tensed. These winter thunderstorms could be fierce. They would need to hobble the horses in a safe place so they didn't break free.

As they set to work making camp, the unrest that had weighed so thick among them these past days faded away with the urgency of the storm.

More lightning flashes came, closer together now, and with the thunder rumbling deeper each time. By the time the first drops fell through the needle-covered branches overhead, they had leathers tied up for covering, a large stack of firewood, and even a low flame licking at the dry logs.

They settled in around the fire, Lola on one side of him and Mr. VanBuren on the other. That had become the usual arrangement, and he was happy enough not to accidentally brush Will's hand as a dish was passed around the circle.

Lola looked to the VanBuren men. "Did you find a safe place for the horses? Most of them were fine in the last storm, but White Owl's mare doesn't like thunder."

He'd taken over Lola's packhorse when he joined on with them. The animal had proved decent, but he missed his old gelding who'd been with him for three winters now. That pony was the fastest he'd owned and could outrun any buffalo. Except that last one.

After they reached the other side of the mountains, perhaps he could hunt enough to trade for a new horse of his own. That way he wouldn't always be riding a mount that belonged to Lola.

His mind had begun to think of continuing with her even after she found her brother. He would accompany her back across the mountains, of course.

But after that? The future seemed blurry. She would return to her home far toward the rising sun. He'd never desired to go to the white man's land. But he'd never known a woman like Lola either.

"We found a little patch of grass surrounded by trees. Figured they could take shelter or graze as they prefer." Will didn't sound as surly as he sometimes did. Maybe the storm had pulled him from his sour mood.

Lola nodded. "That sounds wise. I'm sure your two pack-horses didn't like being hobbled."

Maybe that question was her way of making sure the men had secured them all. They normally let the two remaining packhorses graze freely while the riding mounts were secured so the entire group didn't disappear in the night.

"Indeed, they didn't." The older man shook his head. "I held each one while Will dodged flying hooves."

The rain fell harder outside the shelter, it's loud patter

making it hard to talk. Another crash of thunder came, this time nearly at the same moment as its flash of light.

Lola jumped at the sound, and White Owl staid himself against the urge to shift closer to her and tuck her into his side. Could he do that with the others watching? A glance at the men showed both eyeing him, and the distrust was plain in Will's gaze. Did they suspect his thoughts? Clearly, neither would sit quietly if he moved closer to her. Not even when another clap of thunder made her curl into her coat.

Anger slid through him. Was it because he was so different from them? Probably. Or maybe they simply hadn't known him long enough. His sister had been so young when she died, but if he tried to imagine her grown and a stranger coming in their midst, he could see how it would be hard to watch that man take a place beside her until White Owl knew him to be trustworthy.

Proving himself to these men might be a long and challenging task. He had no need for Will's respect, but the older man—he meant much to Lola. White Owl had to honor him.

Lola glanced toward White Owl, and he met her gaze, doing his best to send his strength without reaching out. The tension tightening her eyes eased a little.

Another flash of light lit the sky like a fireball, and a boom exploded through the air. White Owl's body clutched tight. That had been more than thunder, surely.

A horse's scream sounded over the pounding of the rain. He leaped to his feet.

Had one of the animals been struck? He sprinted into the rain, weaving between trees in the direction the men had returned from after they'd secured the horses.

Frantic animal calls sounded from ahead. One of them must be wounded. *Creator Father, have mercy on it.* He'd never known a man or animal struck by lightning but had seen burn marks in trees.

That would be a horrible way to die.

CHAPTER 12

*T*he sky had grown so dark with the pelting rain, White Owl barely realized he'd reached the clearing until he stepped into the open. He slowed, taking in the scene, searching for the source of the horse's screams.

There. A massive tree lay on the ground, it's needle-covered branches spreading wider than he was tall. Had the tree been struck by lightning? What of the horse?

Will moved past him, and a glance back showed Lola and VanBuren close behind. He needed to find that horse and do whatever merciful act he could.

As he approached the tree, the animal finally came clear. Lying beneath the branches, it struggled to free itself.

Another lightning flash and explosion of sound ripped through the air, this time not quite at the same moment. The horse screamed again. Will had already reached its side and crouched at the head.

White Owl moved around for a better view of how the animal was pinned. This was Will's mount, the animal he rode every day.

White Owl bent low and pushed branches aside. The trunk

was as thick as the length of White Owl's forearm, and it lay hard on the middle of the horse's back. They could push it off, though it might take all three men.

"Help me move the tree off him." He called loudly enough for the others to hear as he dove into the prickly branches.

Gripping the trunk, he pushed with all his strength. His moccasins slipped in the wet ground. The tree shifted, but not enough to clear the horse. Will moved in on the other side of the animal, and together they heaved against the tree again.

The trunk moved more this time, and they should have been able to push it off the animal's hindquarters, but it seemed stuck halfway over the rump. Maybe the roots still lodged in the ground held it.

He eased back to gather another wave of strength. The older man and Lola had taken positions on the other side of Will. Maybe with all of them, they could move it enough to pull the horse free. *Creator Father, let the animal be able to stand on its own.*

Inhaling a deep breath, he surged forward with the others. He was positioned at the thicker part of the trunk, so his efforts would be most important. He had to give everything he had left. Even more than that.

His entire body strained, his head aching like it would explode and his wound throbbing like in the days it had festered. Another clap of thunder bellowed. The horse cried out and flapped his head. It's body didn't move, though.

With the last of their effort, the tree finally shifted. Only the length of a finger at first. He heaved harder. Pushed with everything in him. Gulped in breaths without letting go and strained even more.

The tree moved again, farther this time. It had passed the highest part of the animal's rump, now only needing to clear the knob of the tail.

With one final roar, the trunk gave way enough to free the horse completely. White Owl slumped to the ground, his body empty of all strength, at least for a moment. His arms trembled, and the cold had very little to do with it. The rain actually felt good, it's icy pricks bringing his senses back to life. He gulped in deep draughts of air.

Beside him, the horse still lay there. It lifted its muzzle, an act far more feeble than before. Will seemed just as exhausted as White Owl, but he turned and crawled to his animal's head. Through the ruckus of the rain, White Owl couldn't quite make out his words.

Will grabbed the length of rope fastened as a halter and pulled. It stretched its neck to comply, but it didn't move anything more than a single front hoof. Was it so exhausted from struggling?

White Owl scanned the length of the animal for any other barrier that might be holding it down. Hobbles still fastened around the back legs. They usually secured in the front, but this one had injured a front ankle two days ago.

He gripped his knife and slipped it from its sheath, then leaned forward and sliced the rope to free both hind legs. Surely now it would rise.

Creator Father, give it strength.

A line still pressed across the animal's back and belly where the tree had lain. Not a good sign. Did that mean broken bones? That might be the reason it didn't move its rear half.

White Owl struggled to his feet, then moved to Will's side and reached for the rope. Will didn't release it, but he didn't push White Owl aside either. Together, they pulled on the cord.

"Up, boy! Get up." Will screamed to the animal, then moved one hand to pat its neck for encouragement.

The horse tried, stretching its neck and flailing its front feet in an effort to find purchase. But the back end didn't move at all.

White Owl's belly clenched in a tight knot, but he handed the rope back to Will. "Keep pulling."

He moved around to the horse's rump and fit his hands underneath, helping the animal from behind as it struggled with its front. The back end was a dead weight.

As they tried several more times, Will's calls became frantic. "Up, boy. You have to get up!"

The horse didn't seem able to lift even its head by itself now. They needed to end its pain. That was the only merciful thing to do. Yet Will didn't look resigned to that end.

White Owl looked up at Lola and VanBuren, who stood back, watching the scene. Even in the dim light, with rain plummeting down her face and flattening her hair to her skin, he could see the reddened sadness in Lola's eyes. The older man's grief showed easily in his expression too.

Lola must've felt his gaze, for she looked up at him. A knowing showed in her expression, an awareness of what had to come.

He worked to shore himself up. Will didn't appear able to handle the deed, and he couldn't ask an elder or a woman to do such a thing. That left only him.

Creator Father, if You don't wish to heal the horse, please give me strength.

~

"*D*o you want someone to hold her while you climb up?" Lola had already mounted her own horse as they prepared to set out this morning, but she'd happily slip down and hold the packhorse-turned-mount that Will would be riding if it made this transition any easier for him.

Now that they were only down to one packhorse, they'd rearranged their packs to spread them behind each person's saddle. None of them were certain, though, whether the mare

Will was trying to climb on had ever carried more than a pack-saddle load.

"I have it." Will ground the words through a locked jaw as he tightened the reins and placed his foot in the stirrup once more. The moment he leaned weight on that leg, the horse shimmied away, snorting and jerking its head back against his hold. Will released a few sour words about the mare's gender and disposition.

Lola clamped down her annoyance.

Will moved quicker this time, sliding his foot in the stirrup and springing up onto the horse's back. He barely caught a grip on the saddle before the mare jerked sideways again. When she wasn't able to pull away from the weight atop her, she exploded into the air.

Lola did her best to hold in a scream as the animal bucked and thrashed. She nudged her horse toward the lurching mare, barely daring to breathe as Will clung to the saddle with both hands. His body had slid sideways. No matter how much of a death grip he held, he wouldn't be able to hold on much longer. And the frozen ground would do nothing to comfort his fall.

She reined her horse near the mare, but the crazed animal swerved away from her. That sideways movement loosened the last of Will's grip. With the next buck, he flew free of the horse.

At the last minute, one of the flailing hind hooves caught his legs, whipping his body around just as he slammed to the ground.

Bile rose up her throat as she leapt from her horse and ran to Will's side. He wasn't moving. Mr. VanBuren reached him at the same time, and they knelt over opposite sides.

A groan sounded as Will shifted, then raised a hand to cover his eyes. Thank God he was moving.

"Are you hurt, son?" Mr. VanBuren laid a hand on his shoulder.

Lola moved her gaze down the length of him. His legs

splayed at different angles, but she couldn't tell for sure if they were broken. "Can you move your legs? Does it feel like anything is damaged?"

A groan was his only answer.

White Owl crouched beside her, then placed his hand on one of Will's knees. He wrapped the limb with both hands and slid them down toward the foot, straightening the leg as he went.

Another groan sounded from Will. "Get your hands off me." But his voice lacked strength, and White Owl didn't stop.

He moved to the other leg, starting just above the knee and working downward. A large smear of mud on Will's trousers showed the spot where the horse had kicked him. White Owl slowed when he reached that spot, then shifted his palm around the area.

"Get away from me. Get him off." Will's voice came stronger this time, and he lifted his hand from his eyes to glare at White Owl.

White Owl ignored him once more, moving his hands down the remaining length of leg. Then he pulled back and turned to Will's face. His voice stayed measured as he spoke, no hint of anger from the man's harsh words. "I think nothing is broken. The leg will be sore, but better if you stand and walk on it."

Will struggled to sit up, and Lola and his father reached to help him. He slumped back to the ground before they could do much, laying his hand over his eyes again. "It's my head that hurts, not my legs."

That must have been what struck the hardest. She moved her hand to the base of his neck, feeling beneath his hair as she worked her way around his head. "Do you remember what happened?"

"That blasted horse." He mumbled the words with pain lacing his voice. At least his memory hadn't been affected.

He winced when she reached a spot just behind his left ear.

"You have a bump coming up here. That's all I feel though."

She straightened and sat back on her heels. "It's probably best you lie here a while."

"I can get up. Don't need you coddling." He still kept one hand over his eyes but made a shooing motion with his other.

Lola raised her brows at Mr. VanBuren. Though worry lines etched deep around his eyes and mouth, he gave her a sad smile and a dip of his chin. "I'll sit with him."

She nodded and rose to give them some room. Maybe she and White Owl could catch that rascal of a horse. It didn't seem wise to attempt to ride it again, not when they would be climbing the side of a mountain as soon as they started out. They might need to stay in this place today to give Will time to recover. At least the trees they'd camped under gave shelter.

One more day lost.

But he hadn't intended for his horse to die, and he certainly hadn't intended to be thrown from his mount first thing this morning. Better she not let her impatience show.

White Owl had already caught the troublesome mare and stood holding her near the other horses.

Lola moved to them and took up her horse's reins.

He met her gaze with a question in his eyes.

"We should probably wait here today for him to recover. If he's not injured badly, we can set out tomorrow." She slid a glance to the pack mare behind Mr. VanBuren's horse. "I know she's never been ridden, and her temperament doesn't inspire much confidence." She turned back to White Owl. "Should we try to ride her today and see if she's an option?"

He shook his head, and he seemed to be contemplating something. "You are small. We can ride together. He can take this horse." He stroked the splash of white that marked the face of the mare he'd been riding. The animal leaned into his touch, her eyes closing in trust and pleasure.

Lola's insides were far less relaxed than the horse's. Her heart picked up speed at the thought of sharing a mount with this man. Sitting so close to him, her arms wrapped around him —it sounded too wonderful to hope for.

But some of the trails they'd taken had been almost too steep for a horse with only one rider. "Will it be too much for her?" She stroked her mare's neck.

White Owl's gaze slid over the length of the horse. "I will walk when the trail is hard."

That didn't sound pleasant, but it might be their best option. Perhaps she and White Owl could take turns walking as needed. He'd stopped limping completely now, so hopefully his leg would be up to the challenge. She'd have to watch for signs of pain though.

Between conniving men and stubborn ones, she had her work cut out for her.

CHAPTER 13

*B*y the time Lola helped White Owl unsaddle the horses, Will was up and hobbling around. White Owl carried their food satchel back to the fire ring, and Lola knelt to stir the coals to life. They might all appreciate a warm midday meal.

As White Owl left to gather firewood, Will hobbled into camp, his father at his side. "What are you doing?" It sounded as though he meant his words to be stern, but the pain lacing them turned his voice raspy.

She managed a smile for him. "Starting some meat to boil so we can have stew for lunch."

His scowl deepened. "We're not staying here. Thought you were in a hurry to find your brother."

She straightened. "We should rest today. We can start fresh tomorrow morning."

"The sooner we leave this place, the better." He turned to look around, the action almost wooden because he shifted his entire body instead of twisting his neck. He must have a powerful ache in his head. "Where's that horse? She won't throw me again."

Lola had to work to hold in her sigh. "Sit a while, Will. Please. If you sleep an hour, your head will likely feel better. We can talk about riding on then." The last thing she wanted was to deal with his grumpiness all day.

He spun on her, then winced and raised his hand to cup his brow. "Where's that horse? We're riding now." He spoke through gritted teeth, which might be from pain or anger. Or both.

She rose and stepped around the fire to his side, touching his arm. She used her most placating tone. "You don't have to ride her again. I don't want anyone to. She'll stay a packhorse. Two of us can double up, and she can carry a heavier load of supplies."

He let out a hiss through his clenched teeth. "I suppose you're planning to ride with that Indian." He bit out the word as though he were speaking of Satan himself. "If you do, you'll have taken leave of every last bit of your senses. And I won't be responsible for what happens to you."

Surely it was only the pain that made him speak so cruelly. Yet it took all of her restraint to keep from slamming a palm across his cheek. How dare he slander a good man like that?

She raised her chin. "I assure you, I'm very much in control of my senses. You can ride the mare White Owl has been using. We'll saddle the horses and be on our way." If he was going to be so stubborn and insulting, he could ride with an aching head. She wouldn't force him to go easy on himself against his will.

Mr. VanBuren's face held a grim expression as he helped her and White Owl ready the horses once more. It irked her that he wouldn't put his son in his proper place—or even speak up to recommend a better course of action. But after what he'd said about their relationship, she assumed that he worried that any crosswise word would spread a deeper rift between them.

Mr. VanBuren held Will's new mount while he climbed aboard, and she and White Owl stayed close by.

"Creator Father, give him strength for the journey ahead."

White Owl's quiet voice behind her made her turn. He met her gaze briefly before focusing again on Will as the man eased into the saddle.

Could he really pray for Will after everything the man had said and done to injure him? Though White Owl had left the camp before Will's outburst a few minutes ago, he'd likely still heard the words. Once more, admiration swelled her chest for this man. The strength of White Owl's heart, of his desire to follow Christ, continued to amaze her.

With Will settled, Mr. VanBuren turned to them with a nod, then moved to his own mount and packhorse. Though the day hadn't even reached the noon mark, the slump of his shoulders made him look as though he'd fought a battle. And lost.

White Owl mounted Adelphia in a smooth motion that bespoke much experience in the saddle. Then he moved his left foot from the stirrup so she could place hers there and extended his hand to clasp her arm. Her climbing aboard wasn't nearly as smooth as his had been, but she managed the feat.

She settled behind the saddle, a position that felt both comfortable and foreign. She rested one hand on White Owl's side for balance. His body was as hard as a wood plate, yet tapered to his waist, providing an easy place to rest her hand. They'd moved all the packs off the saddle except their water flasks to give the mare the lightest burden possible.

White Owl rode out ahead as usual, and Mr. VanBuren slipped in behind with his packhorse. Will brought up the rear with the other pack animal. She'd never been so thankful to have her old friend following just behind, for she had a feeling if Will had to stare at her riding with White Owl all day, his anger would be volatile by the time they made camp that night. Who knew what he would do in that case?

Still, was it safe for him to ride behind them all? It would be harder to keep an eye on him and notice if his pain seemed to be getting the better of him. She would have to make sure she looked back often.

They began winding up the side of the mountain soon after leaving camp. The slope was so steep that White Owl led them first one direction at an angle, then the other, climbing ever upward with each step.

When the horses had to scramble up a series of boulders, she leaned forward to speak in White Owl's ear. "Let me walk a while."

He didn't answer but halted the mare and lifted one of his legs over its neck to slide off the side. He landed with a double step to keep from stumbling down the steep slope.

He finally glanced up at her and placed a hand on the saddle seat. "I will walk. You sit here."

She should be miffed at the way he went against her request, but she couldn't deny his gallantry. She'd never had a man go so far out of his way to make hers easier. She shook her head at him but allowed a small smile as she moved into the saddle and took up the reins.

A glimmer touched his gaze, and the corners of his mouth tipped up. "Just don't ride over me."

"We'll do our best not to." She loved the way he teased, the humor almost hard to hear unless she watched his eyes.

White Owl started first up the rocks, climbing with a speed that explained how he'd developed all that muscle. He didn't have to worry about the horses outpacing him. Her mare hesitated at each new boulder they had to step onto.

When White Owl had gone a short ways ahead, he paused to watch them until they'd nearly caught him. Then he continued on. After repeating this pattern three times, they finally reached an easier section. A trail, in fact, that must have been made by animals like the big horned sheep they'd been seeing more of.

When all the horses had reached the trail, White Owl turned as if he would continue walking.

"You ride now." She slid down from the horse's back so he wouldn't try to argue with her. Another half-hour and they would reach the peak. She could manage that much.

He frowned and shook his head. "It's not much farther. Ride."

She strode toward him, making sure not to let any shortness of breath show from those few steps. Goodness, this slope was steep.

When she reached him, she gave him her firmest look and placed the reins in his hand. "My turn to walk."

The amusement in his gaze shone clearly, but she didn't linger to watch it. Just strode past him in the direction he'd been heading.

He didn't argue again.

By the time they finally reached the peak, she could no longer control her panting. She heaved in breaths, but the air never seemed to satisfy. Her head had begun pounding too. Will must be feeling the same pain, but likely a great deal worse.

They paused at the top and stared out at the sea of mountains stretching before them. She'd never felt so insignificant—a tiny speck among peaks that dotted as far as she could see. There was so much grandeur that her chest ached with the beauty.

Too soon, White Owl's soft voice pulled her from the view. "Will you ride with me now?"

She glanced up to meet his gaze, and her heart fluttered as it often did when he looked at her with such affection.

She took his hand and mounted a little more smoothly than she had earlier. And this time, settling in behind him felt like home. She laid her cheek on his back, letting herself rest in his strength for a moment.

"All ready?" White Owl spoke his usual call.

"All's ready here." Mr. VanBuren sounded a bit lighter than he had earlier. Maybe taking in this view had refreshed his spirits too.

As White Owl guided Adelphia down the slope, Lola glanced back and smiled at both men. Will wore a frown, but that was nothing new. He didn't meet her gaze, just stayed focused on the trail ahead as his mare fell in behind his father's packhorse.

It didn't take long to settle into the side-to-side motion of her horse's gait as they descended the slope. White Owl used the same Z-shaped route he had on the climb upward.

A cry sounded behind them, and she spun to see Mr. VanBuren sliding from his mount. Will's horse was riderless, and Will lay in a lump on the hard ground.

Her heart surged at the sight. "Stop!"

White Owl was already halting their mare, and she slid from its back. She reached Will after his father and dropped to her knees across from him. "Will, what is it? Are you hurt?"

He didn't respond at first, just lay crumpled on his belly with his face facing one side.

She pressed a finger to his neck where the blood should pulse. A steady thump pumped there. Thank the Lord.

He groaned, and she eased out a breath. As he tried to roll on his side, she and Mr. VanBuren helped with the effort.

"Where are you hurt, son?" Mr. VanBuren's voice held a touch of panic, and Lola glanced up at him. His face had paled, but not so much that he would soon be their second patient. Hopefully. She rubbed her hand across his shoulder to offer comfort, but he didn't seem to notice.

When she returned her focus to Will, his eyes were still closed but his lips had parted. "Head...hurts."

She scanned the area. They needed to make camp and get him comfortable. He'd clearly done some damage that morning, and who knew what the second fall had inflicted.

White Owl stepped to her side, and she met his gaze. "Can we make camp here? We'll need water too. We have to make him comfortable."

White Owl pointed to a group of low evergreens about fifty strides away. "We can take him there. I will bring water."

"I can walk." Will's words slurred.

If he could simply keep his head up, White Owl and Mr. VanBuren could support his sides. But if Will couldn't manage that, they would need to carry him, maybe using a blanket as a stretcher.

She looked to Mr. VanBuren as she nodded. "Let's try it."

She expected Will to object when White Owl moved to one side and helped him sit up, but Will seemed to have all he could manage just holding his head upright. The muscles in his jaw and throat flexed as they lifted him to his feet.

She fastened the horses' reins so she could lead Adelphia and the others would follow like a long string of packhorses. Then she urged the group as quickly as they could manage over the rocky terrain. She'd like to beat the men to the group of trees and find a suitable place to camp. It would be even better if she could lay out Will's bedroll for him so he could lie down as soon as he reached the place.

But with the tired horses dawdling, she arrived at the trees the same time the men did. Within minutes, she'd prepared a place for Will to rest, and they lowered him onto the bedding. His head flopped, though he hadn't lost consciousness. He groaned as she adjusted his body to lie flat.

White Owl handed her a water flask, and she pulled out the cork. "Can you drink some of this? I'm sure it will help." He would probably appreciate a damp cloth on his brow too. With the sun shining and the trees protecting them from wind, the weather wasn't nearly as cold as it had been before the rain yesterday.

"What can I do to help?" Mr. VanBuren knelt beside her, panic still lacing his tone. He needed something to distract him. She could hand him the water flask and let him care for his son. But men weren't known for their nursing skills. "Can you unsaddle the horses? Bring the food pack to me." Will probably wouldn't be ready to eat. With a severe headache, often the stomach suffered upset. But she would need what the satchel held later.

As she poured bits of water into Will's mouth, he swallowed, his throat making loud gulping sounds. Probably because he lay flat, but his head needed to remain as still as possible.

At last, he turned his face away. "Just let me sleep." His voice still slurred a little, though perhaps not as much as before.

She straightened and studied him. Maybe sleep would help him most. She should ask White Owl to pray. He was likely already doing so.

Did she dare lift her own petition to the Almighty? He might ignore her since she'd avoided Him so long. But maybe if her request was for Will, not herself, He would listen.

It was worth a try. It was the only thing she could think of to help him.

CHAPTER 14

*W*hite Owl had been trying to put this forced rest to good use by hunting to replenish their food supply, but he wasn't sure whether he was of better use away from camp or staying close by.

The longer Will slept the second day, the more Lola seemed to struggle to remain still in the camp. She flitted up and down, flying to Will's side any time he shifted, stirring the pot where she kept a hearty stew warmed for each of their meals. She needed something to keep her hands busy, which was part of the reason he'd gone to hunt. On this barren mountainside, game was scarce, but he'd finally found a small pack of sheep and brought down a ram.

He'd planned for Lola to help with the cleaning and scraping so she'd have something to occupy herself, but as he glanced at the carcass he carried, the sight of the blood made him hesitate. Did white women handle such tasks? Women often took over this work in the Shoshone camps, but he had no idea what happened among her people.

Cleaning hides was hard and messy work. Would she think this a normal activity or would she be insulted?

Knowing Lola, she would make her opinion clear. At least in that he could rely. He'd much rather know her thoughts than always be wondering as he'd been with Watkeuse. She'd spoken frankly enough at times, but he'd never quite understood the routes her mind would take.

He could see the camp now, and Lola had spotted him. She jumped to her feet and paced toward him. The older man sat by his son with a book in his lap. He'd been reading aloud from a storybook when White Owl had left. If it had been Creator Father's Scriptures, he would've stayed to listen. But it was good he'd finally found game.

Lola met him in the trees, her gaze flitting from the sheep to his face, then back down. "You found something?"

He nodded. "A ram. Good meat." He watched her face for this next part. Maybe he shouldn't even offer the task. If it was normal for her to clean and prepare the game, she would simply take over.

But the strain lining her face pushed his words out. "If you wish, you can help cut out the meat and scrape the hide."

Her eyes brightened. "Yes. I'd like to." Then she hesitated. "You'll have to teach me."

So this wasn't work white women did. At least, not women of her station, for *someone* had to prepare their meat.

But if she wished to learn, he would gladly work at her side.

He shouldn't crave so much time with her, but he did. This connection between them was becoming far too dangerous for him. His heart had latched on too strongly to let go when she returned to her people.

She'd said before that he should go on to find the missionaries after they found her brother. Did she still feel that way? If he told her he didn't want to leave her, would it change her mind?

That meant he'd have to make a choice.

～

ill had finally slept enough for his body to heal. Midafternoon on the second day after his collapse, he'd awakened and sat up on his own. After rubbing sleepy eyes, he'd asked for food. Good thing Lola had kept the stew ready for him. He'd risen and walked around that evening, and by the next morning, insisted he felt well enough to ride again. No headache remaining.

His foul mood seemed to have been cured by the long nap also. During the three days since then, he'd stayed quiet, only answering when spoken to. Yet the silence seemed more sober than sullen.

She still wasn't sure if they'd set out again too soon, but Will seemed to grow steadily stronger. At times, he regained that pinched look and grumpy attitude, especially in the afternoons. For that reason, White Owl had been finding camp earlier each evening. But at least they were making progress again.

And a good thing, for it looked like snow would fall any moment.

Lola tucked deeper behind White Owl's back, folding into herself against the piercing wind. They were descending a mountain, not as steep as some, for they were able to go straight down instead of using the back-and-forth pattern. But this one had taken nearly a day to climb, and they'd only ridden halfway down the other side. The peak rose high into the clouds, and they'd just now left the last patch of fog.

If this land they traveled through was considered the easier southern route, she couldn't imagine how hard the Lolo pass would have been. Thank the Lord she'd finally given in to White Owl's guidance.

But with this new snowfall, the danger would increase. Not just the risk of the animals slipping on ice, but the potential for snow slides. Her heart no longer surged when she thought of being buried in that frozen tomb, but she would do almost anything to avoid another such incident.

White Owl raised a hand to point, and she peered around him to see two snowflakes drifting down. Another gust whipped through the air, swiping the crystals from their fall and scattering them far away.

The weather had begun. More flakes fell, growing in steady succession as they stung her nose and cheeks. She could hide behind White Owl and nearly cover herself with her coat, but he sat like a mountain, the icy crystals pelting his face.

This rocky section offered no trees where they could camp with protection. The wind thrashed with a steady strength that made it hard to be heard without yelling. They had no choice but to keep riding, but perhaps White Owl wouldn't have stopped for only a snowfall anyway.

She glanced back at the others. They had both curled into their coats, so she couldn't read expressions. Mr. VanBuren would surely call out if he needed to stop, but Will might not. As soon as they reached an area level enough, she would ask White Owl to halt so they could discuss whether to keep going or somehow make camp.

The snow began to gather in crevices, and the farther they rode, the more often the horses slipped. The wind wasn't quite as strong now. Perhaps the neighboring mountains sheltered them from its full fury, but she could no longer feel her fingers or toes. Her body had taken up a shiver that she couldn't still.

White Owl didn't seem to suffer as much, as if the cold didn't penetrate his buckskins. Perhaps his body had built up a tolerance for these conditions since he'd lived in this area his entire life.

At last, they neared a massive boulder with a ledge overhanging a protected area. Before she could free one of her hands to point, White Owl turned their mount toward it. At last, a place where they could camp and maybe even keep a fire going.

What she wouldn't give for a hot fire and a warm cup of stew. Or steaming water, or anything that could heat her insides.

They reined in beside the overhang and slipped from their horses. She usually dismounted first to allow White Owl room to swing his leg over the saddle, and when she used his grip to slide down this time, she landed on benumbed feet. Her ankles nearly gave way beneath her, and she tightened her grip on his hand.

The sensation in her feet came back with a surge and a hundred needle pricks, but she locked her jaw and stepped away from the horse, releasing White Owl's hand. The first order of business had to be starting a fire.

She fumbled for the flint box while White Owl unstrapped the firewood they carried with them for a situation just like this, when they needed dry wood in a hurry. They had only enough to burn for an hour, so they'd have to find fallen logs somewhere around here, though trees had been scarce. Maybe a little farther down the mountain there would be a timber forest.

Will stumbled over, a tight expression on his face that showed he must be in pain. If he was shivering as much as she, the shakes likely rattled his head until it ached.

Mr. VanBuren brought several blankets and wrapped two of them around his son, taking the third for himself.

When White Owl had a bed laid for the fire, she bent close and struck flint against steel into the tinderbox that was part of the fire-starting kit.

With her trembling, she had to strike five times before she managed a spark strong enough to catch. Though White Owl didn't offer to take the tools from her, she could feel the urgency in his bearing.

At last, they had a small fire kindled in the dry logs. All of them leaned close, shoulders nearly touching as they stretched hands to the flame. They'd built the fire close enough to the rock that it protected the flame from most of the wind, but enough gusts still blew to offset what little warmth the fire could offer yet.

"We'll need more wood soon." She glanced at White Owl.

He nodded. "I see trees downhill. Will bring logs after I find safe place for horses."

Will looked up, his gaze sharpening. "You're not going to tie the horses in the trees, are you?" After the experience with his mount, none of them had been eager to fasten the animals near timber. But the horses needed protection from the wind and snow too.

White Owl lifted a glance around the slope to the right. "I see more rocks. Will find a place to block the wind. Maybe make shelter." He was always a step or two ahead of them. How would they have managed through these mountains without him?

If anything in her life had been a gift from God, finding White Owl surely had been. Yet, the weight in her belly said the damage to her heart that would come at the end of their time together would be far worse than the good of having him along.

She should protect herself. Pull away from him.

After only a few minutes hovering beside the fire, White Owl straightened. "I will take the horses now."

She should help. He'd been even more exposed to the cold than she, so if he could set to work already, she should to. "I'll go with you." Though her body wouldn't quite do as her voice told it.

"No. Stay and tend the fire." White Owl's voice came sharp. They hardly needed three of them to tend this small fire, but he didn't sound like he would be argued with. Perhaps she didn't *want* to argue. At least she could start a meal cooking.

She pulled herself away from the flame long enough to help him remove saddles from the animals. Within a few minutes, she'd pulled out her pot and meat for a stew, then filled the container with enough snow to melt into water. There was nothing more she could do until that cooked. And the wood they'd brought was so dry, it was burning far too quickly. They would need more wood sooner than she'd thought.

White Owl surely wouldn't have time to set up shelter for the horses, then trek down the slope to find trees and bring logs all the way back up before the flame died. Besides, he shouldn't be required to do all the work. She could bring enough wood to last another half hour or more.

She glanced from one VanBuren to the other. "I'm going down the slope to gather logs. Please keep the fire going and make sure this pot stays in the hottest part of the flame."

Mr. VanBuren's brows drew together in concern. "Be careful, my dear." His voice trembled like that of a man twenty years older. Maybe the cold had numbed his mouth too.

She tried to give a reassuring smile, but her face wouldn't form the expression. "I will." Pulling her coat tight around her, she started down the slope.

The trees White Owl had spotted soon appeared as a dark silhouette in the falling snow. The rocky mountainside proved treacherous in some places, with jutting stones partially covered in snow. She had to watch her footing closely, especially in the slippery parts. One of those especially icy sections slid her toward a steep drop-off that fell at least twenty feet. The other side of that ledge looked easier to climb for her return trek up to the camp.

When she reached the evergreen forest, the shelter of the trees protected her from most of the wind. Entering its confines was like stepping from the storm into a quiet house, with only the whistle of the gale sounding from outside.

Her footfalls crunched over lightly-dusted leaves and twigs. Fallen branches lay scattered through the woods, and she worked quickly to gather an armload of the best ones—logs seasoned enough to catch easily, yet not so rotten they burned too fast.

When she'd loaded as much as she could manage for the

climb back up, she stepped out of the trees. The wind gusted against her, whipping her hair and clothing.

She ducked her chin into her collar and trudged upward. When she'd only managed a third of the way, her arms ached to drop part of her load, and her legs protested the steep climb. She'd taken the new route on the opposite side of the drop-off, but this section didn't seem any easier. Every frigid breath she sucked in made her chest ache. She could leave part of her load here and come back for it, but maybe she could get a little farther with all the wood before dropping some.

With so many logs in her arms, she couldn't see the ground immediately in front of her, but she kept her gaze focused a few steps ahead. There must be at least three or four inches of white covering the ground now and much more swirling in the air.

She sidestepped one of the larger sharp rocks that rose up at an angle. A glance up the mountain showed she'd barely made it halfway back to their camp. She couldn't see the place White Owl had taken the horses. He must still be tending them, for if he'd returned to camp and been told where she'd gone, he would have come to help. She had no doubt.

Every step took the last of her strength, but she managed the next. Then one more.

Her foot slipped on a stone she hadn't seen, and she stumbled to her knees, dropping her load in a clatter. She let her head hang low as she knelt, taking in icy breaths. She would leave part of the wood here. Maybe White Owl would come back for it. Or she could after she rested. Hopefully the snow wouldn't have covered it so much she wouldn't be able to find the stack.

A fierce gust slammed into her, nearly knocking her sideways—toward the drop-off. She had to get up to the protection of their camp.

She worked herself up to her feet, then scooped up half the

logs. This was still a full load. How had she carried so much before?

She started forward, the next few steps a steep incline. Exhaustion pushed her down. It might be better to sit and freeze out here. Or maybe she should leave all the wood. She'd brought it half of the way. Others could do the rest.

But only White Owl would help, and he'd already—

As she stepped up, her foot slipped from under her. She screamed as the icy stone sent both feet plunging downward.

CHAPTER 15

*L*ola landed hard with her belly over the logs, sliding downward. The tilt of the rock beneath her sent her toward the drop-off. She released the wood and grabbed for purchase in the snow. Everything she grasped came away in her hand, not even slowing her slide. The rock beneath her was too slippery. She managed to grab one of the logs, digging it into the snow.

The wood gripped just enough to slow her slide. With her other hand, she reached over to the side to find an area not so slippery.

At last, her hand caught hold of a rock that stuck out above the snow. Its rough surface gave her something to grab hold of.

She hung there, flat against the slippery stone with one hand grasping a rock and the other still clutching the log that had slowed her fall. She held her breath as she turned her head just enough to see how far away the drop-off was.

Only one length of her body away. And now directly below her.

Her breath caught in her throat. She had to move over. Had

to get to a place where her feet could find purchase. But for a moment, she let herself lie there, sucking in breaths and gathering strength.

A form appeared up the hill through the swirling snow. A man.

Relief sagged through her as Will stepped nearer. He'd come just in time.

She called out to him. "Be careful. It's slippery."

He must have heard her despite the fierceness of the wind, for he moved over onto a track that would allow him better footholds.

When he drew near, she lifted her hand from the log to reach for him. She didn't dare release her hold on the rock until he pulled her up and her feet found secure ground. She might never be willing to let go of this lifesaving stone.

He crouched just above her precious rock and reached out. Instead of taking her hand, he gripped her wrist. She fumbled for a hold on him, but instead of pulling her up, he gave a hard downward thrust.

A squeal slipped out as she started to slide again. She still clutched the rock with one hand, and scrambled with her other to find something else sturdy to clutch in the snow. Was he trying to make her fall farther?

His hand closed around her other wrist, the one gripping the sturdy rock. Fear coursed through her as a terrible premonition sank in. He *was* trying to make her fall.

Before she could fight his grasp, he pulled her hand away from the rock and shoved her hard. As he released her, she slid downward, fear flaring through her as her hands scrambled for something to stop her descent.

The drop-off. If she slid over the edge, a fall that far could kill her.

She scrambled, groping with hands and feet for a sturdy

grasp on the ice-covered rocks. One foot found purchase, but as her knee bent beneath her, the momentum of her slide tipped her backward.

Her leg twisted, and pain shot through her hip. Her body tipped sideways, rolling down the mountain.

At last, she struck a rock that flipped her upright again as her feet continued downhill. But the stone caught her coat firmly enough to hold her still.

Her lungs heaved as she sucked in breaths. A commotion sounded above, and she strained to look upward. If Will was coming after her again, she would fight this time. He must have lost his mind completely, but she wouldn't let him hurt her.

Not any more than he already had, though she was pretty sure she only had bruises. Nothing broken.

Two men were wrestling where Will had been. White Owl had the man on his back, pressed to the ground. But Will was fighting with arms and legs both.

She had to get up there and help. White Owl might need something, maybe ropes to secure Will. The man had proved a danger, and he couldn't be allowed another chance to hurt them. They had to find out why he'd turned against them.

Against *her*, rather. It made no sense.

Using the rock that had stopped her tumble, she sat upright on the stone. She'd slid or rolled the length of her body at least five times over. But it looked like most of the track had been along ice covering a large boulder.

To the left of that slippery section, there appeared to be a path of snow with enough stones that she would have hand and foot holds should the rock underneath prove slippery. She would have to attempt it.

White Owl had mostly subdued Will, flipping him over to his belly now. He would need help to get him back up to camp with the slippery terrain.

Her legs trembled as she rose up onto hands and feet, then walked her hands up to the next rock. Little by little, she traversed the slope. The snow packed solidly beneath her feet, not slippery at all in this area.

Still, she kept her hands on the ground, gripping rocks every time she could reach one. She didn't dare risk another fall. At least she wasn't as cold as she'd been before. In fact, her body had heated so much that she might be sweating beneath her thick layers. She was wet though, which meant soon she'd be even colder than before.

When she finally reached White Owl, he was watching her with concern marking his features. He knelt atop Will's back and had the man's hands wrapped around behind him. Will's face was pressed into the icy snow. He would freeze before long if they didn't get him up to the fire.

"Are you hurt?" White Owl looked like he wanted to reach out for her. The last thing they needed was for him to let Will go before they had answers.

She shook her head. "I want to know why he pushed me down the mountain though." She glanced where White Owl held Will's wrists together. "Do you want me to get rope to tie him?"

White Owl shook his head. "You go first if you can. We'll come behind you."

Knowing White Owl, he probably wanted to be there to help in case she slipped again. But what if *he* slipped, especially with Will there to cause trouble? Perhaps White Owl's moccasins gave better traction in the ice than her boots.

They managed the rest of the climb without any more falls, and as they neared the little camp under the ledge, Mr. VanBuren stood waiting for them. His brows drew together when they approached. "Why are you holding him?" He hadn't eyed White Owl with such distrust since those first days together, when White Owl had been injured and helpless.

Perhaps he hadn't seen Will push her. He likely *hadn't* from this angle. Will's body would have hidden his actions.

Lola worked to calm her ire. It was time for Will's treachery to be made clear. "I lost my footing on an icy section with a cliff just below. I thought Will was coming to help me up. Instead, he grabbed my wrists and shoved me down the slope. I nearly fell over the edge before I managed to break my fall. I could have been seriously hurt...or killed." She turned her focus to the younger man. "I want to know why."

Will looked positively frozen, snow crusting his face and his teeth chattering fiercely. White Owl still gripped his arms behind his back, which made Will hunch forward. "C–cold. Fire."

As much as she wanted to feel no compassion for the man, she had been almost that miserable only an hour before. She wouldn't wish it on anyone, especially when the fire blazed only steps away.

She looked to White Owl, and he seemed to read her thoughts, for he pushed Will toward the fire. Will stumbled forward, then dropped to his knees by the flames, leaning over them.

Lola moved to the pack that held extra rope. When she carried it toward White Owl, Mr. VanBuren stepped in her way.

"Hold on now. You can't tie him up like a criminal. We need to discuss this. That's my son."

Something in his voice, especially at the end—a hint of desperation, maybe—gave her pause. He was trying to rebuild the connection with Will, and part of that would mean giving the man the benefit of the doubt.

But she'd been there. Felt the panic as Will shoved her down the icy slope. Even now her clothing was soaked from the snow that had tunneled beneath her coat as she rolled down the mountain.

She stiffened her spine and raised her chin to meet Mr.

VanBuren's worried gaze. "He tried to hurt me. He shouldn't be allowed freedom until he accounts for those actions." She moved around him to crouch beside White Owl.

"Wrap it around." He shifted Will's arms to give her access to the wrists, and she coiled the rope around them, leaving one end free so they could tie the other to it.

When Will was bound tightly enough that he could never free himself without flame or a sharp knife, she backed away and moved to kneel by the fire where she could see his face.

The blaze would die down soon, and it looked as if they'd used all the wood. Someone would have to go back and retrieve the logs she'd left on the mountainside. If White Owl volunteered for the task, she might just let him. As long as he promised to take care and not go near the slippery place without a firm grip on a secure rock. Between today's ordeal and the snow slide, she would be happy if she never again trekked through these mountains during winter.

White Owl and Mr. VanBuren also gathered around the fire, though the elder remained standing. He gripped his hands in front of him, maybe simply from worry, or maybe to keep from reaching out to his son. Either way, she hated the position Will's actions placed his father in.

She turned to Will. The others might have questions to ask, but she wanted to be the first. After all, she'd been the one to bring them all here, and it was her safety he seemed determined to endanger. "Why did you do it? Why did you push me down the mountain?"

He didn't look at her, just kept an un-focused gaze aimed toward the flames. His teeth still chattered. He was probably still recovering from his injury. Had the scuffle with White Owl reinjured his head? Or was this simply a ploy for their compassion?

Her own head ached from the cold. Frustration wasn't

helping any. "Answer me, Will. Why did you push me?" Her voice rose, but she had every right to vent a bit of anger after everything.

He finally lifted his gaze, but his eyes looked almost confused. Maybe even sad. "I didn't mean to. I was trying to help you up. When I grabbed ahold of you, my foot slipped and I fell forward. I let go of you to catch myself so we wouldn't both fall. I thought you still had a grip on the rock."

Could he be serious? She replayed the scene in her mind. He'd definitely pushed her. Hadn't he? She'd not looked up at his face, she'd only been focused on reaching his hands. She'd been so relieved, then the fear…

She hardened her resolve. "You pushed me, Will. I'm sure of it. Why?"

His gaze finally sharpened and flicked to his father, then back to her. "I didn't push you. I would never hurt you. I was trying to save you." His voice strengthened as he spoke. He sounded so sincere, his tone more earnest than she would've thought he could manufacture.

He let out a sigh and met her gaze. "Lola, I won't deny I was hoping to earn your…affections. When you rebuffed me for him"—he slid a look toward White Owl—"I was hurt. But I've never, ever meant you harm. I might have wanted to plunge my fist into him once or twice…" His voice gentle as he searched her eyes. "But I would never hurt you. I promise."

Her mouth turned dry as she studied Will. Could he possibly be telling the truth? Had her fear twisted her memory of what happened?

She did her best to keep her thoughts from showing on her face as she looked from Will to his father to White Owl.

Mr. VanBuren's expression beseeched her almost as much as Will's words had. He wanted her to give his son another chance. How could she deny him this request, when she'd wished so many times that her own father would have shown so much desire to connect with her? Would reach out to her and stand up for her against life's frustrations?

When she looked at White Owl, his features had taken on that impassive look, yet she'd learned to see beneath it, somewhat anyway. This time, she could easily see a shadow of anger in the flare of his eyes.

He believed the worst of Will. He'd been the one to speak against him from the beginning. Could jealousy play even a small part in his opinion? Perhaps even without White Owl realizing? He knew Will had shown her extra attentions before. How could that not affect his opinion of the man?

Perhaps she should ask exactly what he'd seen. Maybe from his angle, Will's actions had been more obvious. She kept her voice low and forced a measure of calm into her tone. "What did you see Will do?"

"He held you." He gripped his own wrist with the other hand. "Then pushed." He threw that arm away from himself. "He did not try to help. Only watched you fall."

Only watched you fall. She inhaled a deep breath and blew it out. That was similar to what she remembered. But when she slid another glance at Mr. VanBuren's face, the pleading there constricted her chest even more.

If only she could tell them all her real thoughts. How torn she was. But she had to keep a confident façade with these men. If she showed weakness and Will really did intend her harm, she would play into his plans.

She locked her gaze with Will's and shored up her defenses. "Too many things have happened, Will. Too many coincidences that cast suspicion on you. We can untie you for now, but know you'll be watched very closely." She gentled her tone. "And if there's something I've done to anger you or hurt you, please tell me. I'll make it right, if it's in my power."

She could feel White Owl's anger thickening the air around them. She would have to talk to him. Explain her reasons. But not with the others around.

CHAPTER 16

$\mathcal{I}$t had taken White Owl all night and nearly half of today to calm his anger. His frustration with Lola had swelled until it rose even higher than his fury with Will. The man was a slithering weasel—that fact had been well established. But for Lola to believe him... To accept his whining apology and release him...

White Owl should have spoken up. He should have interrupted when she'd been making her choice. But she'd seen his opinion when she looked at him.

That should've been enough. After that, well... He'd learned with Watkeuse that speaking his mind when a woman had already made up hers never ended well.

He wanted to tell Will that if any harm came to Lola, White Owl would kill the man. But that wasn't loving his enemy.

Creator Father, what should I do? About this man who would bring harm to her, and about my anger toward them both. Though his frustration had eased, it certainly hadn't gone away. And the walls between him and Lola grew thicker the longer they rode. She'd even removed her hands from his side, where she always placed them.

Creator Father gave no sign of an answer, but White Owl waited in silence. Perhaps the words in His book were the way He would give His wisdom. If only White Owl could read those words for himself.

It was late enough in the day that they could make camp. Perhaps there would be enough light that Mr. VanBuren would agree to read aloud for a while. He'd done it the other times White Owl had asked.

He'd been hoping Lola would teach him to read the book once they had more time. But he would have to break down the barrier between them before he could ask.

And he would have to keep her alive.

As they made camp, White Owl kept Will by his side and as far away from Lola as he could manage. She'd permitted the man to walk freely but had made it clear he wouldn't be allowed free rein.

In strained silence, they settled the horses, then gathered firewood to add to what VanBuren had already brought in.

Their entire group had been quiet much of the day, and that lack of talking remained as they ate around the campfire. He would much rather have silence than flared tempers, though the sadness in Lola's eyes pressed a weight in his chest.

When the older man had taken his last bite, White Owl presented his request. "Will you read from the Bible?" That's what he called the book.

VanBuren's brows rose. He seemed surprised every time White Owl asked. White Owl couldn't let himself wonder why. He wasn't sure he wanted to know what that man thought of him. He couldn't allow it to change his own actions. Not when he was doing his best to keep them in line with what Creator Father wished. He'd made the wrong choices so many times in his life, letting his own selfish desires rule what he said and did.

But with Creator Father's strength, he was doing his best to follow His commands. To obey the commands of the God who had shown himself both powerful and good in White Owl's darkest moment.

He simply needed to know what Creator Father wanted in *this* situation.

"That seems a good idea." VanBuren reached for his pack, and his gnarled fingers fumbled to unfasten the tie. Finally, he opened the Bible and leaned near the fire for better light. The sun had not yet fully set, but soon the fire alone wouldn't provide enough light for the older man's eyes.

VanBuren's aged voice trembled as he began but grew strong after the first few words. White Owl strained to focus on each one, to draw out as much of the full meaning as possible, though he knew not the interpretation of some.

"Think not that I am come to send peace on earth: I came not to send peace, but a sword."

What could Jesus have meant with those words? Was he not to love his enemies and pray for those who hurt him, as the missionaries had said? How then should he also take up his weapons against others?

In *defense* of his enemies? That would only make more enemies, who he would also need to fight to protect. It seemed an endless battle. One some of the warriors from his village would appreciate, no doubt. But that didn't settle with the picture of Creator Father he'd understood.

He focused on VanBuren's reading again. Maybe his questions would be answered the more he heard. Some of the language he couldn't interpret, but VanBuren spoke slower as his eyes seemed to struggle with the waning light. "...and he that loseth his life for my sake shall find it."

The man looked up and straightened, blinking twice. "I'm sorry, it's getting too dark for me to see well enough." He glanced around the group, then his gaze settled on White Owl again with a sad curve of his mouth. "Perhaps I can read again in the morning after we break our fast."

White Owl nodded. He would have to content himself with what he'd been given.

But as he laid out his furs and tucked himself into them, he lifted up a silent prayer to the God he was working so hard to follow. *Show me what You would have me do. Make clear to me so I can do Your will.*

He stared up at the stars sparkling between the branches overhead, and the unrest in his spirit eased. For the first time in too long, a bit of the peace from that first time he'd met Creator Father settled around him. Maybe he was on the right path still.

~

*L*ola had to fix this. Had to break the silence that stretched between her and White Owl.

The only way to do that was to apologize to him. Part of her had hoped a bit of time would settle things and she wouldn't have to bring up that awful night and why she'd chosen the way she had.

But he was right not to return to their easy camaraderie. These challenges had to be spoken of. Had to be worked out together. Even if she couldn't have a life with him, she couldn't stand having him so angry with her.

She'd looked for a chance to talk with him alone during their midday rest, but White Owl never allowed Will to stray far from him. Speaking to him without listening ears would be impossible. Part of her wondered if White Owl might also be avoiding her and using Will to help with that purpose. That didn't seem his style, though. He did the hard things when they needed to be done.

Now she must do the same.

It seemed the only way she would be able to manage a private conversation would be to speak while they rode. Will and Mr. VanBuren had moved to riding ahead of them at White

Owl's request, probably so he could keep a closer watch on Will. She should be able to speak quietly enough not to be overheard. The downside to a conversation while they both faced forward was that she wouldn't be able to see his expressions while she spoke.

But perhaps that would be a blessing. She could say what she needed to without having to see whether he accepted her apology until she was finished and he spoke.

If she couldn't clear the air between them, the last few hours before they camped would be uncomfortable. But no more than these last days had been, surely.

In truth, a little discomfort was the least of the reasons why she wanted him to forgive her.

Give me favor with him, Almighty God. Soften his heart.

After releasing a long, quiet breath, she began. "I'm sorry. I know you're angry with me for letting Will go free the other night." She kept her voice low, but the tightening in his body showed he heard her clearly. "If you'll listen, I'd like to tell you why I made that choice. I don't want there to be this wall between us. You are my friend." And so much more. But she couldn't let her thoughts stray that direction now. "You have come to my aid so many times. I don't want you to think I am unthankful. I'm more thankful than I can say. But I need to explain. Will you listen?" It wasn't as if he could run away to keep from hearing what she said, at least not without causing a stir. But she wanted to honor his choice.

And she needed him to speak, needed to hear his voice. To know if raising the topic had angered him even more. Perhaps not being able to see his face wasn't such a benefit after all.

"Yes." The single word barely told her anything. His tone wasn't easy and light as it had been before this debacle. With that single sound, she couldn't tell if he was open to hearing or simply responding because she'd asked the question.

She would have to charge down this path she'd begun and

cease worrying about his reaction until she finished. "I've known Mr. VanBuren as far back as I can remember. He was my father's closest friend."

She paused. "I suppose that's not the place to start the story though. My mother died when I was a young girl. I have no clear memories of her, only a sense of being held, maybe rocked. Though that could've been by a nurse. My father was the only parent I knew. He entrusted my care to nurses and governesses —a long stream of them, so I never got too close to any. Nor to him, looking back. We were always formal, speaking like acquaintances even over the breakfast table." She was using words White Owl might not understand. Perhaps she should summarize this part in a single sentence.

The one that sprang to mind made her chest ache, but it was all too true. "Looking back, I'm not sure I ever really knew my father. And I'm not sure if he loved me, or if I was only a responsibility to him." She'd never voiced that last part aloud. Hearing it now, the sting of traitorous tears rose in her throat.

She inhaled a settling breath and released it. "Mr. VanBuren visited our home often through the years, and he was always warm and pleasant. He spoke of his son sometimes. Will's mother had also died when he was a boy, and Mr. VanBuren sent him to boarding schools—places where he went to live and be taught by others. I think Mr. VanBuren really thought that would be the best thing for his son. It wasn't until Will was nearly grown that he realized they barely knew each other. Not like a father and son should be. When I spoke with him that night after the incident by the waterfall, he said that before I asked him to travel west with me, he'd been trying to get Will to come for a visit. This journey was his first real chance to get to know his son. To love him as a father."

Her stomach knotted, and she swallowed down the nerves attempting to clog her throat. "I see Mr. VanBuren trying to help his son. Trying to stand up for him and show his love, though it's hard for a man who's spent so many years squelching those desires. The other night, I saw him doing for Will what I wish my father had done for me."

Once more she swallowed, this time to loosen the ache in her chest. "I couldn't get in the way of that. I had to give them a chance."

White Owl didn't answer right away. Maybe he thought she wasn't finished speaking. But she'd said everything in her heart.

Help him understand. It wasn't fair of her to send so many pleas heavenward when she and God hadn't yet talked out their differences. Maybe if things went well in this conversation with White Owl, if he offered understanding and forgiveness, she could find courage to have the same type of conversation with the Almighty.

Long moments passed as the trail they followed descended the final slope of a mountain and crept along its base through a path between trees. Animals must use this trace often for the ground to be so worn.

At last, White Owl shifted in the saddle, turning nearly halfway around so he could look at her. She searched his face for any sign of his thoughts.

Instead of the impassive expression she'd expected, a host of emotions clogged his gaze. So many, she couldn't decipher them all.

When he spoke, his voice rumbled low, no trace of anger in his tone. "I know what it is like to not have a father. This, maybe Will and I share, in a way. And perhaps it is as hard to have a father but not know his love. I understand why you wish to bring them together. But I cannot. I cannot give him another chance to hurt you. I hope that you can understand."

As he spoke, different layers of his emotions seemed to step forward in his gaze. Sadness. Longing. Understanding. Anger. Determination.

Now, what shimmered there looked awfully close to hope.

Hope that they could compromise. Could return to the easy way that had been between them before.

She wanted that even more than he could understand. It would end soon enough, when they reached Caleb's camp, but until then she would take every moment he offered.

She kept her gaze locked with his as she dipped her chin in a nod. "I understand, and I'm very glad."

CHAPTER 17

"Only two more mountain ranges? Really?" Lola gripped White Owl's sides tighter to keep from bouncing on the horse's back. "How many days do you think that will take?"

He glanced back, enough that she could see the way a corner of his mouth tugged in a grin. "Three sleeps to the grassland, then two more to the Nimiipuu village." About five days then.

They were nearing the end. She could finally find Caleb. Meet the half-brother her father had loved enough to give so much of his estate to.

Caleb wouldn't know their father had died, not unless one of the many people she'd spoken to while she searched for him had traveled ahead to give him notice. But one would have to be quite a devoted friend to journey such a distance simply to give him the news.

Or to warn him? To prepare him so he could plan how to take over her part of the inheritance as well? She had no idea what this brother was truly like, only that he'd once become a minister. But that profession hadn't lasted very long. Now he was married to an Indian woman and had a child with her. The pieces didn't form any puzzle that made sense. She would simply have to wait and see.

And she was more than thankful to have White Owl with her for the meeting. Mr. VanBuren, too, though he'd distanced himself from her these past days. It didn't seem like he and Will had drawn closer though. In truth, the older man, the person she'd always considered like an uncle, had shriveled into a weary, saddened version of himself on this journey.

Perhaps she shouldn't have asked him to come. She certainly shouldn't have allowed him to bring along Will. She'd had no way of knowing that before they left, though.

White Owl's hand closed over hers where it rested on his side, as though he could read her thoughts. He always had a way of knowing when she needed his nearness.

The more time she spent with this man—the more long days they had in the saddle, talking, sharing simple touches, the more she saw of his integrity, his desire to follow the God he'd so recently met—the more her heart had fallen for him. She didn't deserve him, this she knew with every part of her mind. He was too good, and she had been bitter for so long, it had surely tainted every part of her.

But that didn't seem to matter to her heart.

Could she work hard and become the woman he needed?

But it was more than that. He deserved a woman who sought God's heart, who wasn't clogged with bitterness toward the Almighty. She *wanted* to be that person, for White Owl but also for herself.

Yet there was so much that still separated her from God. These frantic pleas for help she kept sending up weren't fair to Him, not until she'd settled all that lay between them.

She had to do it. She couldn't move forward—not with White Owl, and not even on her own—until she did this hard thing.

The incline the horses had been tracking up leveled off a little, and White Owl called to the men ahead of them. "Halt. Stop to rest."

Will glanced back, then he spoke to his father ahead of him.

As both men reined their horses in, White Owl slid to the ground. He glanced up at her, his eyes softening as their gazes met. "I will walk."

She'd long ago stopped trying to take a turn at walking. It seemed to frustrate him when she insisted, and as often as she did other things that irked him, she could happily give in on this count. Perhaps he liked the chance to stretch his limbs. He never seemed short of breath like she was after only a few steps.

While they let the horses stand for a few minutes, White Owl repeated to the others what he'd told her. Two more mountain ranges. They were so close.

At last, he pointed out a route up the remaining slope. "Follow that line of rock to that ledge. Then turn."

"All right." Mr. VanBuren patted his mare's neck. "You ready, girl?"

The older man set out first with his packhorse trailing. Then Will and his own pack animal—the one that'd proved unsuitable for riding. He'd insisted on keeping charge of her though. Men could be so stubborn about the appearance of admitting defeat.

White Owl motioned Lola ahead of him so he could bring up the rear.

As they rode, she glanced back occasionally to make sure he wasn't falling behind. His long strides traveled the same speed the horses did, even up this steep slope. By now, they'd nearly traveled three quarters of the way up the mountain. Using this back-and-forth pattern took longer, but none of their animals could have plunged straight up, especially in the thick snow and ice covering the incline.

A few scraggly trees clustered beside the trail, just enough to block her view of the landscape around them. She'd seen enough majestic grandeur these past weeks for the beauty of these mountains to seed itself deep within her. As much as she hated the cold and dreaded the thought of another snow slide, she couldn't resist the way the majesty inspired and renewed her.

They reached the final steep climb before the ledge where they would turn, and she leaned low over the saddle as Adelphia struggled up the slope. The mare's rear hooves slipped, but she scrambled forward, lunging up the incline. *Come on, girl.* Lola strained to help the horse in any way she could, though there wasn't much she could do from the saddle.

At last, the mare stepped up on the small plateau. The other horses and the VanBuren men waited for her, saving just enough space for her mount to stand on level ground.

Her horse's sides heaved as they both struggled to catch their breath. No trees edged this flat area, and she stared out at a breathtaking view. Peak upon peak rose as far as she could see, an endless vista of snow-covered majesty. The sight soaked into her soul as she took in each mountain's unique shape. She was so small, so insignificant among all this God had created.

She'd been petty in her life, thinking that the way she'd given God the cold shoulder all those years gave her the upper hand. He had created all this, imagined it and spoke it into being. If He wanted a part in her life, who was she to say no?

In truth, her heart wanted very much to say yes.

Yes, Lord. Be not only my Creator, but my Father too. Peace settled in, soothing her spirit, easing the unrest so she could finally breathe. She took a deep inhale of the cool air, letting it weave through her and bring her to life. God had planned even this, the way their bodies took strength from the air around them. *Guide me, Lord. Teach me how to become the woman You intended long before my birth.*

A presence stepped beside her, and she glanced over at White Owl as he rested a hand on her mount's neck.

His eyes were soft as they met hers, as though they understood something had just changed within her. Did it show so easily? Maybe not. White Owl always seemed to see deeper than others did.

Still, she *wanted* everyone to see this change in her. Wanted witnesses to keep her accountable on her new path.

She glanced over at Will beside her, but the fierce expression on his face caught her breath. The anger. It flashed away, covered by a stoic look that made the other seem like a dream. Had she really seen such rage in his eyes?

A lump clogged her throat, and she swallowed, taking in another breath of the fresh icy air to bring back the joy from moments before. *God, what have I done to him?* He must have seen the exchange between her and White Owl. He didn't have to have real feelings for her to be angry that his suit had been thwarted.

Yet White Owl had been right. That look must have been what he'd seen early on, what had prompted him to accost Will at the falls. She would have to apologize when they were alone. If they ever managed that feat again. Possibly not before they reached Caleb's village.

On the other side of Will, Mr. VanBuren's saddle squeaked as he straightened. "I guess the horses have caught their breath. Are we following those tracks up the slope?" He pointed at a line of tiny hoof prints in the snow that traveled approximately the same angle they'd just ridden, but in the opposite direction.

"*Ha'a.* Yes."

She loved when White Owl slipped some of his native language into his speech, though he didn't often do it when the other men could overhear. He must be weary now.

As Mr. VanBuren's mount and pack horse moved past them

to start up the trail, she caught White Owl's gaze. "Do you want to ride?"

He shook his head, his eyes taking on resolve. Were all Shoshone men as strong as he? If so, whatever training they received should be brought east for use on lads in the States.

She had a feeling some of White Owl's strength came from his own character. And how much of it was being molded by his new faith? Maybe together they could grow. She had the knowledge of the Scriptures and Christianity, yet not the character she wished for. White Owl had developed that character, but not the foundation of knowledge. They could each help shore up the other's lack.

Could it be possible? Could a life together work? So many questions remained. So many details would need to be considered. But for the first time, a life with this man didn't seem completely out of the question.

He stepped back, resting a hand on her horse. "I will return." After moving down the trail a few steps, he slipped in behind a large rock. He must need a private moment.

"Why don't you take this pack animal for a while, Lola. She's dragging my horse down." Will reached back and began unfastening the tether strap attached to his saddle.

"I suppose I can." It seemed he'd finally had enough of the animal. It wasn't very gentlemanly of him to foist a burden off on her, but she didn't blame him for wanting to be rid of the horse. Besides, Lola was in charge of this expedition. That meant everything was ultimately her responsibility.

The pack mare stood on the other side of Will's horse. "You'll have to come around and get her. There's not enough room behind for her to turn." He motioned to the open space in front of them.

She eyed the area between them and the drop-off. There was enough room for her horse to walk safely, as long as she didn't shift sideways too far. Adelphia was well mannered, so crossing in front of Will's horse shouldn't be a problem. And they'd followed trails on ledges narrower than this. It must be the open view that made this feel so unprotected.

She nudged her mare forward and turned in front of Will's mount, giving it just enough room that the animals wouldn't fight. She slid a glance over the cliff. She'd not been close enough before to tell if it dropped straight down, but she could see clearly now. The cliff fell sharply for a long way, at least halfway to the bottom of the mountain before a small bit of snow-covered rock jutted out. Then small evergreens grew from there to the base. A wash of dizziness swept through her.

"Wait."

She turned away at the sharp bite in White Owl's voice and had to blink at the swirl in her mind from peering so far down.

A shout sounded beside her, and she spun toward the sound. A force slammed into her leg —Will's horse pushing her. Her mare stumbled sideways toward the cliff's edge.

Panic clutched her chest and she screamed, kicking her horse forward to get past Will's animal. What was Will doing? Her mare struggled to move out of the way as Will's mount shoved them sideways.

Why was he forcing the animal?

They'd nearly reached the drop-off, and she clutched the saddle. She had nowhere to go—the ledge on one side and a charging horse on the other.

Shouts sounded around her, but she focused on clinging to the saddle and spurring her horse forward. If they could somehow get away from the pressure of Will's horse pushing them...

Then his animal pulled back. Lola's horse scrambled forward, kicking snow over the cliff as she fought to lunge clear of the edge.

Anger sluiced through her, replacing the terror from a heart-beat before. This was it. Will had clearly tried to send her and her horse to their deaths over the cliff's edge. When they reached safer ground, Lola turned to see what in the world had just happened.

Yet Will no longer sat atop his horse. Two men grappled on the ground, half covered in the thick snow.

Dangerously close to the edge.

She sucked in a breath as a new rush of terror choked her. White Owl. Which form was him?

His black hair came clear as he rose up to plow a fist into Will.

The glitter of a metal blade flashed in Will's hand. He plunged it upward as White Owl struck the side of his forearm, deflecting the blow.

She couldn't scream again, not with no breath flowing through her. But she had to help.

Her rifle. She gripped the stock and jerked it from its scab-bard, her trembling fingers clumsy with the movement.

When she lifted the heavy gun to aim, the scene before her made her entire body go numb.

The men were at the edge. They wrestled fiercely, Will's hands around White Owl's throat and White Owl clutching Will's shoulders. The knife had disappeared, but blood marred the snow. Crimson everywhere.

Bile rose in her throat. She had to stop this.

She raised the gun to sight down the barrel, but shouts broke through her focus. Mr. VanBuren. He ran toward the men, waving and yelling.

Will lay nearest the edge, and she could only see his face, twisted with the effort of squeezing the breath from White Owl's throat. His expression, the rage and strain, swept through her with a new urgency.

She squinted down the barrel, focusing her aim on Will's

outstretched body. White Owl's legs blocked part of her view. She'd have to get this right.

Before she could pull the trigger, White Owl rose up until he was nearly on top of Will. A roar sounded as Will rolled him sideways, toward the cliff's edge.

She tensed and pulled the trigger.

CHAPTER 18

$\mathcal{T}$he gun slammed into Lola as the explosion sounded. Black powder clouded around her.

Only one man lay on the snow, motionless.

Her heart seized as her mind scrambled to accept what the sight meant.

No. It couldn't be. If Will lay on the ledge, White Owl must have...

She gripped the gun and jumped from her horse, then sprinted toward the drop-off, lifting her feet high to make it through the snow.

Will was sitting up as she dropped to her hands and knees to peer over the edge. She couldn't worry about him now, not until she knew about White Owl. Maybe he was clinging to the cliff and needed help.

As she strained to see down, her vision swam and her middle swooped. She pressed her lips together to still the roiling, then focused on the snow halfway down.

There. That dark form. Was that White Owl? A sob rose in her chest.

He wasn't moving. How could this have happened? The

strength drained from her body and she struggled not to collapse in the snow. How could she have lost him? This couldn't be.

"Pa, what are you doing?" Will's voice broke through her pain.

She swallowed. Squeezed her eyes shut. *Lord, give me strength.* This debacle wasn't over. She couldn't let herself grieve until this was finished. And she had to get away from this murderer, put some distance between them.

She still had a loose grasp on her rifle, though it lay beneath her hand in the snow. She opened her eyes, tightened her grip, and pushed herself upright, then scooted sideways away from Will.

When at least ten feet separated them, she raised her gun to firing position and finally turned for a real look at the man. She should fear him. He'd tried to take her life—had succeeded in taking White Owl's. But she didn't have the energy for fear, only the hatred that was rising like a mountain in her chest.

But he already sat with his hands raised away from his body, eyes wide as he stared back toward the horses.

She twisted to see what had alarmed him.

Mr. VanBuren stood by Will's horse, rifle positioned to shoot—aimed at his son.

"Are you hurt, Lola?" The older man's voice rasped, but it held more steel than she'd heard from him in months. He must've finally found the strength to realize the truth.

And even the courage to face it head on.

"I'm not hurt." Her voice sounded hard, so filled with iron that no emotion could break through. If only her insides could be the same. "But White Owl is dead." Those words. How could they be true? How could she live with their truth? She wasn't sure she wanted to.

Mr. VanBuren's gaze hardened. No hint of affection or even

pain lived there. "I can't fathom why any decent man would wish to take another's life, especially the life of a woman and a good friend of our family. In fact, a woman I've considered like a niece for many years now. Yet I saw you do it with my own eyes. I watched you throw that honorable man off this cliff. And I want to know why."

She forced her gaze away from this man who made her want to both cheer and cry. And turned her focus to the other, who made her want to spit. And scream. And sob for a very different reason.

Will sat almost motionless. Blood smeared his cheek and nose, though she couldn't see any cuts there. More blood marred his coat sleeve over his upper arm in a circle about the size of her fist. His coat was torn too. Maybe from a knife or perhaps her bullet. She didn't care much at the moment.

Only his words mattered, if he would speak the truth at last. The resolve that took over his features gave a little hope he might.

"I did it for you." His voice didn't waver as he spoke to his father.

Mr. VanBuren's tone held just as strong. "If you think I would want you to kill her, you don't know me at all."

A hard sound came from Will—a laugh with no humor attached. "And that's the problem, isn't it? You don't know me either. You don't know that I owe more money to creditors than your entire estate is worth. You don't know that I've nearly lost my life more times than I've tried to take hers on this trip. I finally have the chance to get away from it all. To pay them off and be done. All I have to do is get her out of the way." He sent a hard look toward her.

Her? His words made no sense. Who would want her out of the way?

"Why? Who would want you to hurt her?" Mr. VanBuren's voice vibrated a little, losing some of its steel. His brows lowered, and it looked as if his hands holding the gun trembled a little. Maybe not. It was hard to tell from this distance.

"The man who owns the sporting club. I take it he knew her father or is involved with his business somehow. I didn't ask questions, not with what he offered me."

Did this man want her father's estate? Did he think that, if she were dead, he could somehow get it all? She knew so little of Father's affairs other than what had been laid out in the will. What of Caleb? Perhaps that was a question for Will. "Are you also supposed to kill my half-brother?"

He slid a glance her way, but came nowhere near meeting her gaze. "He never said anything about that." Perhaps the man planned to deal with Caleb's portion another way. Maybe try to pretend he'd died or couldn't be located.

"Why did you say you're doing this for me? It sounds like you've got yourself in quite a fix." Mr. VanBuren's voice sounded weaker than before. Was that sweat on his brow? Hearing his son's situation must be hard for him.

Will's voice softened. "I was planning to move back to Pittsburg. To move in with you, if you'd allow it. You've been asking me to come. I thought this might be a fresh start for us."

Mr. VanBuren's rifle trembled in earnest now. His mouth parted, but he couldn't seem to find the words. Her chest ached for him. It was what he'd been hoping for, but not like this. Not at all like this.

His lips closed, then opened again. A sound came out, like he was trying to speak but couldn't. A ripple of alarm spread through her. Was something wrong with him?

Before she could stand and move to his side, his knees buckled. He crumpled to the ground.

"Pa." Will lunged forward, nearly sprawling on his face as he tried to stand and run. He ended up crawling on hands and knees, though he favored the bloody arm.

Another sob burned her throat, and this time she couldn't

keep it down. Was she to lose everyone she loved on this mountainside? She had no one left, not her father, not White Owl, and now she would lose Mr. VanBuren.

She pushed up to her feet but had to hold out her arms to steady herself for the first step. The rifle felt impossibly heavy in her hands as the shock of everything stole most of the strength from her limbs. Then she reached Mr. VanBuren's side and knelt opposite Will. The man's eyes were cracked open, but moisture dotted his brow.

He looked from his son to her. What could she do for him? Her mind couldn't focus. Her body felt numb. She reached up and stroked his hair back from his face.

His eyes drifted closed as though relishing the touch. The act seemed to panic Will, for he gripped his father's coat. "You can't leave me, Pa. You can't leave me. Not now. You're all I have left."

That made two of them. Though she hated to have anything in common with this lecherous snake.

Mr. VanBuren's eyes opened, his gaze moving to his son.

Will stilled, the strain of whatever was happening to Mr. VanBuren nearly smothering them both.

She needed to get Mr. VanBuren a drink. Maybe water would help. But her body wouldn't move.

His lips parted like he would speak. He seemed to be trying to, and she leaned closer to hear him. His eyes roamed to her face, hung there, softening. She moved her hand down to take his.

Then his eyelids lowered again. His body went still.

Her heart froze as a numbing weight pressed down on her. *No.*

She had to be strong. Couldn't let herself think about what was happening. Maybe he hadn't died, though certainty settled deep inside her.

Still, she pressed fingers to his neck where lifeblood should pump. She held her breath, straining to feel something. Anything.

No pulse thrummed there. She pressed her lips together, squeezed her eyes shut. He was gone. God had taken one more person she loved. The last one. *Why?*

And he'd left her with...

She forced open her eyes. Forced her gaze to lift to the man crouching across from her. As she focused on Will, the rage on his face nearly made her draw back.

"You," he spat. "You thief. You Jezebel. You stole my father all those years ago. And now you stole him from me again. No matter the money. It's time you pay."

Like a coiled viper, he lunged at her.

She had no time to scream, or grab the rifle she'd laid across her lap, only to raise her hands as a shield. He barreled into her. With one hand on her wrist and the other on her shoulder, he slammed her backward. She fell into the snow, his weight on top of her.

For half a heartbeat, he pulled away, and she gathered herself to fight back.

But then his hands closed around her throat, his weight pressing around her.

Terror surged. She couldn't breathe. Memories of being entombed in the snow flared through her mind. The weight of it pressing on her chest. Her face.

But this was so much worse. The pain of his weight at her neck, crushing her.

She tried to scream, but no sound would come. She gripped his upper arms, fighting to push him away. Her arms weren't long enough to reach his chest. From this angle, she had no leverage to fight him off.

Terror merged into certainty. She would die like this. In the same position that had given Will the upper hand over White Owl.

Her chest heaved to breathe, but the air couldn't draw past the clamp around her throat. Her body was nearly to the point of exploding.

Gray clouded her vision and darkness circled around the edges.

This was it. Her end. At least she wouldn't have to grieve those she loved. She could join them.

I'm coming, Lord. Tell them I'm coming.

~

*W*hite Owl pulled himself up onto the trail with the last bit of strength he possessed, then slumped onto the snow. His head pounded and his throat ached, but he had to get to Lola. If that snake had already hurt her...

Shouts sounded from ahead of him, and he worked to lift his head. That was Will's voice.

Only the top of the man's body showed above the uneven terrain. Just enough to see him spring forward as though charging at someone.

Lola.

Rage flared through White Owl, infusing him with a rush of strength he shouldn't have had. He pushed up to his hands and feet, needing all four limbs to scramble up the trail the horses had traversed not long before.

His vision blurred as his head pounded with the effort. But he had to get to Lola. *Creator Father, give me strength.* He wouldn't be able to help her with what little of his own power he had left.

As he cleared the top of the trail to reach the flat area beside the ledge, he paused to take stock of what was happening.

VanBuren lay flat on the ground, and beyond him, Will knelt over something. Lola.

A rush of new strength charged through White Owl as he stood and sprinted toward them.

Will glanced back at White Owl, surprise marking his face.

White Owl had no weapons. He'd lost his blade and tomahawk in the scuffle before. But he had his hands and the power of Creator Father.

That was all he needed.

He plowed into Will, knocking him away from Lola. The man fought like a cat, a fact that had surprised White Owl earlier.

Will squirmed partway out from under White Owl's hold and reached for his neck. That was the move Will had tried before, but White Owl was ready for those surprisingly long arms this time.

He chopped the grip aside with a hard side arm, then grabbed the man's shoulder to flip him onto his belly. That would be the way to subdue this snake.

But just like a cat, Will wriggled down, squirming halfway out of White Owl's grasp.

White Owl scrambled to lock hold of the man, finally gripping his chin and a chunk of hair.

But with a fierce kick, Will landed a heel in White Owl's gut.

He sucked in his breath and stilled himself against the pain.

Will took advantage of the distraction. He pulled free of White Owl's hold with a yell, leaving hair in his grasp. The man truly did fight like a wildcat.

White Owl turned to face a new attack. He needed to find a knife or some other way to slow this scoundrel down.

But Will wasn't charging toward him. He scrambled on all fours, trying to get to his feet in the snow. Was he going after Lola again? She hadn't moved, but White Owl couldn't let himself think about whether she still lived. He had to deal with this killer once and for all.

Will finally surged to his feet just as White Owl gained his own. The man sprinted past Lola, toward the ledge.

Fury balled in White Owl's chest. He must be trying to lure White Owl there so he could throw him over the cliff again.

Not a second time.

He needed a weapon. He spun, searching the snow around him. There might be a rifle on one of the saddles, but he didn't have time to find it.

There. Beside VanBuren. The older man's body still hadn't moved, and it had lost all color, taking on the lifeless look White Owl had seen too many times.

He worked to push aside the pain of that realization and reached for the rifle. *Creator Father, let there still be bullet and powder loaded.*

As he spun back to face Will, he raised the gun to aim and fire.

The other man stood at the edge of the cliff, staring down, as if taking in the lay of the land below. Wondering how White Owl could have survived such a fall?

Only by Creator Father's mercy could he have landed in the one spot padded by thick snow. Sharp rocks protruded on both sides of him as he'd scrambled along the cliff wall until he reached a place to climb upward.

Will looked back at White Owl, watching him as White Owl raised the rifle and squinted down the barrel. He couldn't see the man's expression well as he aimed, but the piercing rage no longer twisted his features. This was more like an overwhelming sadness.

White Owl hardened himself and fingered the trigger. Before he could squeeze, Will turned back to the ledge and jumped.

CHAPTER 19

*P*ain pressed in White Owl's chest. An emotion he never would've expected. Not for the death of a man who'd tried to kill both White Owl and the woman he loved. This ache must be placed there by Creator Father, a small shadow of what He felt at the death of one He'd created.

White Owl needed time to think through this feeling, to speak to Creator Father about these things. But first he had to check on Lola. See if she lived. He would see to VanBuren as well, but he was almost certain nothing could bring the man awake again.

Keeping a firm hold on the rifle, White Owl dropped to his knees beside Lola. Her eyes fluttered open, hazy in their depths.

Hope flared through him, and he brushed the hair from her brow. She still lived.

But her throat. Maybe that dark skin was a shadow from her coat, but when he pushed the edge down, a nearly black line circled all the way around her neck.

A new rush of anger churned in his belly. His own throat ached from the hands that had gripped it, the thumbs pressing in to the tender parts.

He wanted to stroke her bruised skin, but his touch might bring more pain.

Instead, he shifted to look into Lola's eyes. Her gaze asked questions her throat might not allow her to speak.

White Owl brushed his thumb across her cheek. "He's gone. Over the cliff." His voice came out in a raspy whisper, and even those few words burned. "I need to go see if he survived the jump. Can I do anything for you?"

She shook her head. Moisture made her eyes glisten, and as her hand came up to cover his, a tear crept down her temple. Whether from pain or the awfulness of what had happened here, he wasn't sure. Probably both.

He leaned down and pressed a kiss to her brow. "Stay here." With a final stroke of his thumb on her cheek, he pulled away and pushed to his feet. Now that passion no longer surged inside him, his body was again feeling the effects of what he'd been through.

He had to make sure Will wouldn't climb up and surprise them. With the rifle in hand, he trudged to the cliff's edge.

He searched the landscape below for a long moment before his eyes found the figure sprawled at the base of the first trees. The legs flared at odd angles, and no part of him moved. He must have struck one of the sharp rocks and been flung against the tree.

White Owl pressed his mouth shut against the churning inside him. This man, too, had been created by the One who made and loved White Owl. How must Creator Father be mourning the loss of one He'd had great hopes for?

A sound behind made him turn, his body tensing. Lola had risen and was walking toward him. Not staying where he'd told her to, though that shouldn't surprise him. She certainly knew her own mind, and that was one of the things he loved about her. Perhaps she also needed to see this to ease her worries.

As she stepped up beside him, her hand found his, weaving

their fingers together. He held tight to her. After all that had happened, only Creator Father could bring them to this point, where they both lived and could stand on this precipice together.

She stared down for several breaths, then she leaned in to White Owl, pressing her shoulder against his. His body craved the same contact.

Releasing her hand, he wrapped his arm around her, pulling her even closer.

Their journey wasn't over, but they'd made it this far. Surely they could face whatever lay ahead.

~

"*D*o you think that will be enough?" Lola laid the last of the rocks they'd gathered over the body of the man who'd meant so much to her throughout her life. She stepped back and studied the pile as White Owl repositioned one of the stones.

"Should be." He stepped back to her side and examined the mound. "I will bring more tomorrow. Here and down below."

She nodded. White Owl must be beyond exhausted. And probably hurting even more than she was. Like her, he'd been nearly choked by Will's long arms, but White Owl had also been thrown over a cliff.

Still, he'd gone down on his own and covered Will's body with stones. What they'd done here would be sufficient for the night.

The image of Mr. VanBuren lying in the snow slipped back into her mind. His skin had been ashen, nearly as white as the ground around him. Yet that hadn't been him anymore. Though his body lay under these stones, his spirit was rejoicing in the wonderful place God had prepared for him.

Her heart ached. She wanted to be happy for him, but the way things had ended... *Lord, why did it have to end so?*

Maybe she shouldn't have brought him out into this mountain wilderness. But then she wouldn't have met White Owl. Even now, his hand brushed against hers, their palms meeting, their fingers threading together as they stood at the cliff's edge. *Thank you, Lord, for giving me Your strength.*

A verse threaded its way through her mind. *And God shall wipe away all tears from their eyes; and there shall be no more death, neither sorrow, nor crying...* That had been somewhere in the New Testament, maybe in the book of Revelation. Perhaps she could find it. This might be a chance to teach White Owl about the Christian's view of death.

She gave his hand a squeeze, then slid her fingers from his. "I'm going to get his Bible. There's a passage I want to read."

She moved to the horses, who still stood patiently in the wide section of the trail. They needed to be tended—unsaddled and fed. That would come soon, after she read from Mr. VanBuren's Bible.

Her fingers hesitated as she picked at the tie on the pack. It still felt so wrong to open Mr. VanBuren's personal things. She would have to sort through them eventually. Will wasn't here to take over. What other close kin did he have? She knew of no one else.

When she lifted the flap, the three books lay atop. She moved *The Pickwick Papers* aside to reach the Bible underneath. The novel's pages flipped open to the paper marking his place.

It was an envelope actually, and her gaze glanced over the writing even as she told herself not to look. But the words, *For Lola*, jumped out at her.

Her breath caught, and her eyes drank in the rest of the message scrawled in her father's lazy hand. *For Lola—in the event she doesn't meet the one-year deadline.*

She reached for the paper, her fingers trembling as she tried to grasp it. Her father had left a message for her? Why was it in Mr. VanBuren's pack instead of with the solicitor?

Her eyes burned as she held the page up. White Owl must have realized something was amiss, for he'd come to stand at the horse's head. She turned to him, and the tears no longer stayed back.

She sniffed as she held up the envelope. "It's written by my father. The note says it's for me if I don't meet the one-year deadline." White Owl knew about the requirement, but would he remember the details?

But he was nodding, understanding easing the worry lines on his face.

She studied the writing again. "Am I allowed to open it now? Or do I need to wait until the end of the year?" She nibbled her lip. She still wasn't certain whether she would make that deadline or not. There no longer seemed as much urgency to maintain ownership of their home. Did she even want to return to Pittsburg? What would it be like to stay in this wild country?

As White Owl's wife. Even the thought flared heat through her.

She looked to him for any sign of an answer. He regarded her carefully, almost hesitantly. "It is yours to decide. If my father had left a message for me to read after his death, I would wish very much to know his words."

The earnestness in his gaze made her want to step into his arms. He'd lost both parents so young. Of course he would crave anything from them. Especially a message specifically for him.

If she allowed herself to feel it, her own heart yearned for the same. As much as she'd resented and even hated her father for the things he left in his will—the shock of learning about Caleb and his mother and the way her father had so callously added the requirement that might leave her homeless and penniless—she still craved the papa she'd always wished for. Even the man she'd lived with, the one who spoke to her as to a business associate instead of a daughter, but at least he'd been present in her life.

In that way, she'd been blessed with far more than Will. Far more than White Owl too.

She swallowed the knot in her throat, then used the side of her hand to wipe enough moisture from her gaze to read.

Her fingers still trembled as she broke the wax seal and unfolded the papers. The entire page was full of her father's scroll. Three pages actually, though the third looked almost like a separate letter with its own greeting and signature.

She focused on the first.

My Dear Lola,

A sob choked out before she could stop it, and she pressed a hand to her mouth. He'd never called her *my dear*, not even in the letter he'd left with the will explaining about Caleb and his mother.

Why now, in this note she might never have seen if she'd succeeded in her mission? For these two words alone, she was so thankful she'd opened the envelope.

Again, she had to wipe tears from her eyes to read.

I need to tell you now what I was unable to say before, not even in the letter I left with my will. I was too ashamed, in truth. Too ashamed to own up to the error of my ways. You might have noticed that in my other missive, I only shared the facts about Caleb. Him, I can't regret, though I greatly regret my actions in breaking ties with him. I'm sorry if that point hurts you, my girl.

I'm sorry, too, for all the pain I brought you upon my death, and for all the ways I failed you during my life. I know I wasn't the father you needed. I wasn't good at fatherly words or touches, or telling you how I really felt about you.

God has seen fit to allow me this one last chance as I lie here dying, and I must take it.

You have always been the light of my life. Coming home to you, sharing conversations, hearing of your studies and your wide variety of interests—I always marveled that the Almighty had entrusted your care to my hands. I'm sorry I never told you how much I love you. How proud I am of you.

I'm also sorry that I failed where Caleb was concerned, maybe even more so than with you. At this point, as I take my final breaths, I can't make up for not being there for him, for not somehow finding a way to be part of his life, even when his mother sent me away. But I can do what I'm able upon my death.

It's important to me that he know he is equally my son and has been loved all these years, though from a distance. That's why I left half of the estate to him.

Don't be angry with me, Lola. Please.

I've ensured there will be plenty for you to maintain the lifestyle you're accustomed to. I also hope you'll find a young man you can love and respect, and who will adore you as much as I have, but will be much better at showing his affections. Please tell your future children their grandpapa loves them, even long before their birth.

If you're reading this letter, it means you didn't find Caleb. Or at least that you weren't able to return with his signature acknowledging his inheritance by the end of the year. I had so hoped the two of you would get to meet, and that he would be the brother you should have always had. Once more, I regret how deeply I failed you there.

You'll remember the will stipulated that your inheritance would be forfeit should you not return with your brother's signature within the year, and my entire estate, including our home, would be donated for an art museum. I'm sure that made you angry, but I hope you will forgive the liberty. I needed to ensure you would do everything you could to find Caleb.

Enclosed with this letter is a document you may give our solicitors overriding that portion of the will. I have always meant for you to remain in our home as long as you wish. I would not take that from you, my dear.

I have created duplicate copies of this note and the official missive to the solicitors, and I'm entrusting one set with Ike VanBuren. The other I will leave with the solicitor's office. If Ike is around, I have asked him to make sure he's the one to place this letter in your hands. He has been a good friend to us both through these years, and I know he will be a support to you if you happen to feel any grief at my passing.

There's so much more I wish to say, my dear. But my strength begins to wane.

Know that I love you, and I look forward to our meeting again in the wonderful home God has prepared for us both.

Your loving papa

ears streamed down her cheeks in steady streams, and her insides felt both numb and aching. This letter sounded nothing like the man she'd known. Or at least nothing like the man she'd convinced herself her father had been after she heard his will. Had she really been the light of his life? Why had he never said so?

A sob jerked through her chest, and White Owl's arm around her tightened, pulling her closer to him. At some point he'd drawn her near, and his strength now sheltered her.

He must think her weak with all these tears, and right now that was true. He murmured quiet words into her hair, words she couldn't understand, though their sound wrapped around her like a soothing blanket. Maybe he would teach her his language if she asked.

For long moments, she stayed there, letting the contents of

the letter become real in her mind, allowing White Owl's care to support her.

At last, she sniffed to slow the stream, then glanced at the last paper. As he'd said, it was a letter addressed to the solicitors and dated the night before he passed. The details changed his earlier will, leaving everything he owned to her if she didn't find Caleb. It also suggested Ike VanBuren be engaged as a business manager to help her navigate her new holdings.

Pain pressed in her chest again. She no longer had Mr. VanBuren. But at least she had her father's love. It seemed she'd had it all along.

And as her mind's eye swept back over scenes from her growing up years, she could see little ways he'd showed his affections, now that she looked at them through the lens of his letter. He'd always listened to her with patience, no matter what she spoke about. He'd never shuffled her off when he was in the midst of paperwork. He'd never made her feel that his business was more important than her. In fact, she felt like simply another form of business to him.

But perhaps that was because work was all he knew. He'd loved strategizing and chatting about any manner of topics related to his investments. Giving her that same type of interest was his way of showing that he also loved *her*.

Oh, Papa.

She inhaled a strengthening breath, then released it. White Owl still had no idea what the letter contained, but he'd been so patient. Lending his strength and not pressing for her to share her news with him.

She leaned just far enough away to see his face. Worry clouded his dark eyes, and he searched her expression. She smiled to show him the news was good, though the effort tugged at her puffy eyes. She must look a sight. "He says he loves me."

White Owl's gaze softened. "Of course he does."

Those few words, spoken with such conviction, were nearly her undoing once more. Fresh tears sprang to her eyes, but she wiped them away with a little laugh. "I didn't know it. But he said he always did. That I was the light of his life."

A sparkle crept into his eyes, and his mouth curved as though seeing her happy made him happy.

She slipped her hand into his. "Let's finish setting up camp, then I'll read you everything."

CHAPTER 20

"Is that it?" Lola tightened her hold on the reins as she stared at the row of lodges rising in the distance. Her mare raised her head, and Lola loosened the reins, giving the horse a pat.

"That is the village."

She eased out a long breath. It seemed a lifetime ago she'd set out to find the brother she'd just learned of. Now she was finally going to meet him.

Hopefully.

Unless he'd moved on from this place, in which case they would have to keep riding. She glanced at White Owl, and he met her look. Strong and steady. Her anchor through this last week since the VanBuren men's deaths.

It had felt like she'd lost her father all over again, too, receiving his letter and learning he was indeed *not* the man she'd always thought him to be. He was better.

But he was still just as gone from her life.

Yet she had his letter. And his home, too, if she wanted it.

That thought, of course, made her glance at White Owl once more, though this time she tried not to be as obvious.

He felt something for her, that was clear in the way he looked and spoke to her. The brush of his hand in passing, that warming in his eyes and the gentle smile he saved only for her.

But they'd not spoken of how deep either of their affections went. They'd not talked about anything past finding Caleb. Did White Owl still plan to search for the missionaries? She would be happy to go with him if he asked her to.

Could she really be contemplating marrying him? But he was *White Owl*. The man whose heart and faith and strength she admired more than anyone else's.

He treated her exactly as her father had hoped for in his letter—as though he adored her. As though he *loved* her.

Yet they'd known each other less than a month. Perhaps more time was in order.

Besides, her focus had to be on Caleb now. Would he hate her and her father—*their* father?

That seemed the most likely feeling if he'd been raised to think he'd been abandoned by the man.

A group of children scampered from the lodges into the open area in front of the village. Four little figures, and there two women strolling after them. One of the women held a babe in her arms. At least, she held a bundle to her shoulder that looked like an infant.

The children saw her and White Owl, and all paused to watch their approach. The little ones appeared to range in age from perhaps two or three to maybe five years. Or five summers, as White Owl would say.

They were close enough to make out faces now, and she glanced at White Owl. "Do you know any of them?"

He was studying the group. "The white woman was with those who came to my camp."

She jerked her gaze back to the adults. She'd not realized it from a distance and with the native dress, but the woman who held the babe did indeed have light brown hair. Hope stirred in

Lola's spirit. "So she knows Caleb? Do you remember her name?"

"Not her name. She is married to a Blackfoot man."

Excitement coursed through her. A white woman married to an Indian? Perhaps this lady would give her an idea of what such a life would be like. If love alone would be enough to carry them through the adjustments and compromises that would surely take place in such a union.

The children scampered behind the women, and by the time Lola and White Owl reined in before them, a man had joined the group.

He was the one to step forward and address White Owl, though his brows had lowered in a troubled expression. Not anger exactly. Maybe worry? He raised his hand in greeting. "*Behne.*" That was the word White Owl had taught her for hello.

White Owl nodded in response. "Behne." Then he switched to English. "I am White Owl and this is Lola."

The man responded in her language too. "I remember you from the Shoshone camp where we found Watkeuse. I am Beaver Tail. You bring us news of her?"

Watkeuse. The woman who had taken his niece to care for as her own. The woman White Owl had said he might have married. Did he still wish he had?

But he looked relaxed as he offered a single nod. "She is well. Has returned to her village with the two white men who were with you." He turned his gaze to Lola, and the warmth in his eyes laid to rest her concern. He finally looked back at the man before them. "We have come to find Caleb, the one who traveled with you."

Beaver Tail's brows rose. "You have business with him?"

White Owl looked to her, letting her decide how much she wanted to tell this man. Her presence would be a shock to her half-brother. Maybe if she gave him a small bit of warning, he might not be as angry. It was only fair to offer a little advance notice. Well, none of his parentage had been fair to him, but she would make sure her actions were.

She stiffened her spine. "I am his half-sister. I come with news of our father."

~

*L*ola walked beside White Owl as they followed the man Beaver Tail into the village. The two women and the children came behind them, and theirs weren't the only curious gazes that made her skin itch.

With each step, men, women, and children paused in what they were doing and turned to watch them. Some only sent quick glances, then pretended not to look again. But most didn't try to hide interested eyes.

This village reminded her much of the Blackfoot camp she and the VanBurens stopped in before turning south. But something about this place, these people, also made her feel as if she'd stepped into another life. At least two of the men they passed had light brown hair, though their skin was nearly as dark as the rest. Spending so much time in the sun had darkened her own complexion too.

She glanced sideways at White Owl, and he met her look with a softness in his eyes that eased the unrest within her. They would face this together. Both the gawking of these strangers and the coming meeting.

If there hadn't been so many eyes watching, she would have slipped her hand in his, as she had so many times these past days. Whenever sadness pressed, his touch always bolstered.

From a lodge ahead, a man stepped out, straightening to a height taller than most around him. His broad shoulders struck a chord within her. The way he flexed them, as though adjusting himself within his skin. It was like watching her father again, though he wasn't sitting in his desk chair or in their dining room. The surroundings were so very different, but this man had to be...

Her mouth went dry, and even more so when the man's gaze locked on her.

Caleb.

But then his focus shifted to a woman with a long black braid who stepped to his side. She was one of the two who'd been with the children outside the village. Caleb leaned close as she spoke to him but was distracted again when a little body pummeled against his legs. The pair looked down, and a smile washed over Caleb's face as he reached a big hand to ruffle the black hair on the child.

His wife and son? The boy took after his mother a great deal.

Caleb turned back to the woman and spoke a few words.

Then his gaze lifted to Lola, awareness marking the action. His wife must have told him what she'd said to Beaver Tail about Caleb being her brother.

Did he know about her? Would he be angry? The questions that had been plaguing her for five months now would be answered at last. Her nerves knotted in her middle. She didn't want to know the answers, not anymore.

Something brushed her arm, then White Owl's strong hand settled at the small of her back. She took in a deep breath, then released it.

She had no control over Caleb's reaction to her, but God knew how this meeting would go. He had power over the outcome, and He'd given not only His spirit to bring peace, but White Owl to lend strength when she had so little of her own.

Together, they approached Caleb.

Beaver Tail had already stepped aside and was watching them, as was everyone else.

She honed her focus on her brother, doing her best to block out the rest.

Caleb's expression didn't appear angry, more like curious.

When they stopped before him, his gaze moved to White Owl and he nodded a greeting. "White Owl. Pleasure to see you again. I understand you bring good news about Watkeuse."

A movement from the woman beside Caleb snagged Lola's notice. White Owl had said his wife was a cousin of Watkeuse, hadn't he? She was studying White Owl's face with an intensity that seemed to pull an answer from him. She must be worried.

"She is well. Settled in the village's winter camp with my brother's daughter. The two men you sent, Hugh and Louis, are with her."

As White Owl spoke, the deep timbre of his voice drew her gaze to him, as it always did. And as before, he showed no sign that Watkeuse meant more to him than someone he knew. Caleb was watching him intently though. What did he look for?

She didn't have time to decide if he found it or not, for Caleb turned his gaze to her. His eyes roamed her face. Her mouth went dry once more. She needed to speak, but words wouldn't come.

"Hello, I'm Caleb Jackson. This is my wife, Otskai." He drew the woman to his side with an arm around her waist. "And our son, River Boy."

Introductions. She could do that. She'd been trained to the tiniest detail. "I'm Lola Carson."

He blinked. Was it the last name? She pressed on. "I'm your half-sister."

~

*C*aleb Jackson studied the newcomer who'd just shifted his world a bit. Half-sister. He'd never known his father, but perhaps he was about to learn something of the man.

Yet this lady who stood before him looked more shaken than he was. *Help me show her Your grace, Father.*

A glance around at all the curious faces told him what he

should do next. They needed a quiet place to talk, to find out why she'd come and where their father was. *Who* their father was.

Everything.

Otskai spoke before he could put words to the thought. "Come into our lodge. You must be hungry and tired."

He gave her side a gentle squeeze to say thanks. She was always at least a step ahead of him. He stepped aside for Otskai to lead the woman into their home, but before White Owl could follow her, Caleb caught his attention. "Your horses?"

Beaver Tail spoke up. "Adam and Joel are seeing to them. They will bring your packs to you." His gaze asked Caleb whether he would offer these people lodging for the night.

Of course he would. He nodded. "Have them bring everything to our lodge."

As Beaver Tail left, White Owl turned again toward the lodge, so Caleb spoke quickly to stop him. "Watkeuse. She is truly well?" Perhaps there was more about Otskai's cousin that the man hadn't wanted to share in front of everyone.

Caleb had only met this fellow once before, when they'd gone across the mountains to the Shoshone village to bring Watkeuse back with them. White Owl had been hard to read then, but one thing had been clear—he'd been smitten over Watkeuse. Had something finally developed between them?

The tiniest hint of a smile glimmered in the man's eyes. "She is well. She has…a surprise for you. About the man you sent with her, Hugh. I think she will come to tell you herself when the warm days are back. For now, she and my brother's daughter are in good hands."

Hugh? For the second time in a matter of minutes, the picture didn't fit quite the way he'd expected. "Hugh and Watkeuse?"

The smile in the man's eyes only deepened, though still nothing touched his mouth. He dipped his chin in a single nod.

"I traveled with them part of the way back to our village. I have found him to be a good man. A good match for her."

So that was it. And White Owl seemed fine that he wasn't the one who'd won Watkuese's affections. Caleb searched his face for any lingering bitterness, but his eyes seemed at peace. Much more so than before.

"I'm glad to hear it. Thank you for watching over them, Pop-pank too. My wife has been worried about her cousin. We'll look forward to their coming in the spring."

White Owl nodded once more and turned to enter the lodge. He seemed awfully eager to join the women. And perhaps that had something to do with the pretty lady he'd escorted here—Caleb's sister.

Half-sister, she'd said.

But they could leave off the *half* part. His entire life, the only family he'd had was his mother, and she'd worked herself so ragged it seemed he'd barely had her. He would welcome every new gift of family God gave him.

He lifted his gaze to the sky that was becoming dusky in the early evening light. *Your mercies are new every day, aren't they, Lord? Thanks for this one. Help me be the brother she needs.*

As he absorbed the peace that talking to the Father always brought, he stepped toward the door to their home. It seemed their family was growing even faster than he'd expected.

CHAPTER 21

"*I* never imagined he'd be so...nice." Lola sat beside White Owl on the river's bank, their legs hanging over the edge. The water ran low enough that their feet dangled above the surface.

They'd spent the morning getting to know her new brother and his wife and son. Caleb wouldn't hear of being called her *half*-brother. "He seems eager for everything I tell him. Not angry with our father at all, at least not that he shows. I just keep thinking how much they both missed because Papa agreed to step out of his life."

White Owl's thumb brushed across the back of her hand as the rest of his fingers clasped hers. "You both missed much without each other, but it is good to know him now."

She glanced up at his face. Was he thinking about his own brother? "I'm sorry I didn't get to meet Yagaiki."

His mouth formed a sad smile. "He was the best of brothers. Creator Father did good to give him to me for so long. I am thankful." Then a teasing twinkle touched his eye. "I am not sure what he would think of you. I think he would say I have met my match."

His match. If only those words could be true in every way.

He seemed to realize what he'd said, for his gaze grew serious, locking with hers. "What will you do now that you have found him?"

That was an excellent question, and so much of it depended on White Owl. Would he be willing to take a risk with her? To see what could become with them?

"I, um..." Her mouth went dry with the intense way he watched her. "I told Caleb of the inheritance. He was surprised. He said he's happy here and hadn't planned to go back east. He wants to talk with Otskai and maybe some of his friends before he decides what to do."

White Owl's brows rose. "He might choose not to take his part?"

She shrugged. "He didn't say that exactly, but that's what I think he meant. I'm not certain though."

White Owl was studying her again, which meant he realized she hadn't answered his question. Before he could ask again, she needed to turn it on him. "What of you? Will you resume your search for the missionaries?" Her hand in his began to ache. She'd been squeezing him too tight.

She loosened her grip and turned her gaze to the river.

Yet she could feel White Owl watching her as he spoke. "I would like to help them tell of Creator Father. To speak their words. I also want to learn to read the Bible. I did not realize how hard that would be."

She managed to send him a smile. "You're a quick study though." These last days on the trail, they'd been giving each other lessons, spending evenings and mornings pouring over Scriptures as she fumbled to teach him to read English. Then in the saddle, he would fill her with Shoshone words until her mind could contain nothing more. Since she'd read her father's letter, there hadn't been such a pressing need to hurry, so they'd taken their time with the remaining journey.

She couldn't remember happier days than these last few, though the shadow of the VanBuren men's deaths still hovered, and grief would press through her at the most unexpected times. In those moments, White Owl would hold her, wrapping her tightly in his arms if they were in camp, or clasping their hands together if they were riding.

She was fairly sure it was her grief that had kept him from anything more tender. That one kiss felt so long ago. When her mourning eased, would he attempt another? She would certainly be willing.

While her thoughts consumed her, he'd also turned his gaze to the flowing water. It seemed his own thoughts had done the same. What was he considering? Did she dare ask? Perhaps that was the only way to know him better.

She stroked the back of his hand with her thumb, keeping her touch light, not the stranglehold of before. "What are you thinking of?"

He turned to look at her, and this time his gaze seemed uncertain. Not a look he often wore. "You will need someone to go with you on the journey to your home."

A wash of hope spread through her, as well as a bit of surprise. "You wish to go east to the States?" Was it only for her, or was he also interested in seeing America?

"You will need someone to travel with you." The statement sounded stronger than before.

Was he offering to come only for her protection, or for more? A smile tugged at her mouth, but she tried to hold it in. "And what if I wish to stay here? At least for a while. Maybe longer. Would you go search for your missionaries?"

Now a grin toyed with his own mouth, and his gaze twinkled. "I think it is better we both speak plainly." His dark eyes softened in that special way. "I never thought to see myself with a white woman as wife, but I think Creator Father has brought us together. When I look back at our journey, I see His hand guiding. I asked Him if you are part of His plan for me, and I feel peace." He pressed his fist over his heart.

His other thumb caressed her hand, and his expression grew earnest. "My people are used to traveling. I can make my home in almost any place. I will give you time to know me better. To decide if this is what you want. If you are willing, I will stay with you in this place until you choose what you wish to do next."

Joy swelled so thick in her chest that the ache stole her breath. This man. How could he be so good and still want her? *Lord, you have blessed me indeed.*

Though she'd lost so much, she'd found a whole new life she could never have imagined.

She swallowed the clog of emotion and let her smile bloom. "I am very willing."

~

"*I*t looks like winter has come to the plain."

White Owl nodded at Adam Vargas's words as the hunting party all warmed their hands by the fire outside Caleb's lodge. They'd gone out on an early hunt, this group of men who seemed as close as brothers. Two of them—Adam and Joel—were brothers by blood, but Caleb, Beaver Tail, Chogan, and French seemed to share nearly the same connection.

He'd seen their camaraderie before, when they'd come to retrieve Watkeuse. He'd been a little envious of it then, especially with his heart so raw after Yagaiki's passing. He never would have thought he would now be in this Nimiipuu camp, just like one of them.

He wasn't *quite* like one of them. But since he and Lola had arrived at Caleb's lodge, this group had taken them in. Made them feel almost like family.

"I'm sure winter has long come to the mountain country."

Beaver Tail looked to White Owl. "You said you did not come through Lolo Pass?"

White Owl shook his head. "They wished to, but a snow slide fell on us the first day out. We turned to the southern route instead."

French gave a low whistle. "We've all experienced Lolo pass in the winter. It's not easy to survive, even when your body's accustomed to the cold."

Caleb nodded. "We were sorry to hear about Lola's friends. I'm sure their deaths were hard for you all."

The man looked so earnest, and he had a way of speaking that felt like he really meant his words. His manner was almost always relaxed. He was impossible not to like.

White Owl nodded. He and Lola had agreed not to tell the events that led to the deaths, only that the two men Lola came with had died on a snow-covered cliff.

"I appreciate you bringing my sister west. What are your plans now?" Caleb sounded genuinely interested. He hadn't told yet what he planned to do about the inheritance, at least not that White Owl knew.

Maybe this was a time to ask him. "That depends on you. Will you go east to claim what is yours?" Perhaps he shouldn't be asking this, especially not in front of these others. But if Caleb gave a hint of his intentions, Lola would like to know.

Caleb's gaze shifted to the distance, and he took a moment to respond. "I don't think I'm ready to go back east just yet. Not for another year at least." His gaze flicked around the group and turned a little sheepish. "Turns out we'll be having another little one in the spring."

A hoot sounded from one of the white men, either Adam or French, and even Beaver Tail's face split into a grin.

Caleb's mouth stretched into an impossible smile. "We're pretty excited." He seemed to be trying to rein in his pleasure and return to the conversation. "Anyhow, I figure it'll be at least a year before we think about traveling that far. But even then, I'm not sure I want to go east. I know I definitely wouldn't want to *stay* there. Otskai agrees." He scanned the faces around him. "This is our home. Our family. There's surely enough excitement here to keep things interesting."

He turned back to White Owl. "I'm planning to sign the paper so Lola can claim her portion of the inheritance, although she has the letter from our father saying it's not needed. I'm thinking about giving her my part too. I had planned to talk to her about that later this morning."

Lola would have it all? How could she resist the chance for so much? White Owl couldn't hold her back. From what she and VanBuren had said throughout the journey, her father had left behind a great deal—enough to supply many families.

"Does that help you know better what your next step will be?" Caleb looked at him expectantly, as though the answer he'd just given should make everything clear.

He answered as honestly as he could manage. "I'm not sure."

~

*W*hite Owl stood at the river's edge when Lola found him later that morning. He'd seen Caleb pull her aside, which was when he'd sought the solace of the water's murmur. It was the same mistake Lola had once made, though. The flowing river only helped him think more, not less. And the direction his thoughts took brought pain.

But he was determined. If Lola wanted to return to her home, he would take her there. And he would do his best to stay, if he could manage it.

She came to stand beside him, though she didn't slip her hand into his like she usually did. Maybe the wind that gusted along the water's edge made her keep her fingers tucked in her coat.

"Caleb said he told you his decision." Her voice was soft, giving him no notion of what she'd decided.

He nodded but didn't speak. Just kept his gaze on the flowing current.

"I can't say that I blame him for wanting to stay here. This land has a way of planting itself within a person, taking over a piece of your heart so it might be impossible to be happy anywhere else."

Did she mean *she* felt that way too? She'd only been here a short time, probably not long enough for her to love these mountains the way he did.

She was looking at him now, and he forced himself to meet her gaze. Her face gave no sign of what she would say next, so he waited.

"I don't want to go back either. At least not anytime soon. Maybe I'll return for a short time if Caleb does. But I don't want that life anymore. I've never been so happy as these last few days with you. I want to know my brother better. I want to find the missionaries with you. There's so much left to do here." Her eyes glimmered, her look so full of love that it made his chest burn with the same emotion. "I want to do it all with you."

Joy surged through him, so much that he couldn't contain it all. He finally let himself lean down and brush her lips with his. She tasted even better than he remembered, and he savored the feel of her.

With Creator Father's blessing, this would be the first of a lifetime of more.

EPILOGUE

"Ican't believe you're leaving."

Lola glanced at her brother while she tied off the end of her braid. She would have smiled if not for the ribbon still clamped between her teeth.

"I just got a sister, and now she won't even stick around." Caleb's grumbled words spread warmth through her. Even in her imaginings, she hadn't allowed herself to hope her brother would be as wonderful as Caleb had turned out to be.

Otskai straightened from where she'd been working by the fire and waddled to Lola's side, draping a beautiful buckskin shawl over Lola's shoulders. "I agree that we will miss you, but I am happy for you both. What adventures you will have, translating for the missionaries and seeing all the different peoples. This is the time to travel, before children start to come."

Heat flushed up Lola's neck at that thought. They would come, Lord willing.

"Children haven't stopped our adventures." Caleb sounded offended, and Otskai turned to rub his shoulder.

"Of course not, my brave man." She reached up to press a

kiss to her husband's cheek, but Caleb caught her with a hand around her expanded waist and dove in for her lips.

Lola turned away to give them privacy. She'd had to put up with these kinds of affectionate displays all winter as she lived in their lodge. But the sight reminded her now of what would be coming in just a few minutes.

White Owl. Her chest ached to find him, to feel his solid presence under her own hands. To press her ear against his chest and hear his heart beat. Were they really going to do this? It wasn't the marriage that planted apprehension in her—she'd been longing for it far too long.

But they were leaving this village that had come to feel like home and setting out to the north, to a place neither of them had ever gone. To find people only White Owl had met.

This land was so vast, what were the chances they would actually find the missionaries? Perhaps as great as the chance that she'd been able to find Caleb when she came West. If she'd known how immense this land was then, she might never have attempted it.

Thank You for my innocence, Lord. God had made that journey fruitful, in the greatest sense of the word. He'd brought her together with White Owl, and now they were about to set out on their own mission, to find the brother and sister who'd shared Jesus with White Owl and translate for them so others might also hear of Him.

She'd been working all winter to learn languages. Shoshone first, and the hand signs all the tribes in this area knew. She'd been trying to learn Nimiiputimpt as well, the language of the Nez Perce.

Much of the translation work would be up to White Owl, but she wanted to help as much as she could. She'd had no idea he could speak some of four languages, as well as the hand talk. Shoshone, of course, and English, which he'd become quite fluent in. Also enough Blackfoot and Nimiipuutimpt to carry a conversation.

"You ready, sis? White Owl's waiting." Caleb had torn himself away from his wife and moved to Lola's side.

She turned to face him and took a steadying breath.

His eyes softened as they roamed over her. "You look almost as pretty as Otskai did." When Otskai had offered her own buckskin wedding dress and beaded shawl for this special day, Lola had been excited. But she'd second-guessed herself so many times. Through the winter, she'd taken to wearing buckskin dresses and leggings like Otskai and most of the other women here. Their warmth had been practical, and the clothing made her feel a part of the rest.

But should she have worn one of her older dresses instead? It felt a little like she was pushing away that part of herself, the part she'd been for twenty-five years. As much as she loved these past months here in the Nimiipuu village, and as much as she was committed to becoming White Owl's wife, the path God had led her on to this point had developed her into who she was today.

Caleb still studied her, and a line formed between his brows. "Seems like there was something I was supposed to give you." Then his face lit and a twinkle touched his eyes. "That's right. White Owl said you might want this."

He reached into a pocket Otskai had sewn into his buckskin tunic and pulled out a gold chain. When he opened his hand to reveal the round object attached to it, her breath caught. "The watch."

"He said he took it from the pocket of the older man who traveled with you before he buried him. He planned to give it to you right away, but then he couldn't find it in the saddle pack where he'd tucked it. I guess when he was packing this week for the two of you to leave, he found it pressed into one of the seams."

Emotion burned her throat. What a perfect gift for this perfect day. She took the pocket watch and opened it to reveal the clock face on one side and the simple inscription on the other. *What matters most.*

Tears blurred her eyes as she looked up to Caleb. "It belonged to our father. He left it to Mr. VanBuren."

She closed her hand over the watch and pressed her fist against her heart. This gift came from the two men who'd helped raise her.

Except... Caleb had nothing of their father's. Not even a letter, like she did. Why had she not thought to bring anything of Papa's on this journey? She'd not been thinking of him very kindly when she left, and she'd also expected to return home forthwith.

She held out the piece. "Would you like to keep it? A gift from our father?" She could give this up for her brother. Just seeing it again was enough, the reminder of the two men she'd loved first.

Caleb shook his head, a smile curving his mouth. "You keep it. You're gift enough for me, a lot more than I ever expected."

A new rush of tears flooded her eyes, and she stepped forward to wrap Caleb in a hug. "How did I ever get lucky enough to have a brother like you?" She spoke the words into his shoulder as his arms came around her.

∾

*W*hite Owl stood at the river's edge. Waiting.

Having so many people crowding around made him want to fade into their midst. He never had liked being the center of attention, but he would suffer it for Lola. If only she would come soon.

The women had prepared a feast for the wedding, which was the usual way of celebrating a marriage among his people, and with the Nimiipuu too. But Lola had also wanted them to speak words together in front of all, and for Caleb to speak words over them. This was good, being married before Creator Father.

If only she would come.

The voices in the crowd fell silent, and he looked toward Caleb's lodge. A single figure stepped through the opening and walked toward them.

Not Lola. Otskai's waddle was hard to miss these days. But surely her presence meant Lola would be next.

Another figure stepped out. Caleb, this time. Then he stepped aside for someone else.

Lola.

She straightened with a bearing that bespoke confidence, a look she wore so well. She placed a hand on her brother's arm, and together they walked toward him.

People separated to allow a clear path for them to walk. As Lola drew near, her gaze locked with his. His chest ached with love for her. She was so *tsanavuinde*, beautiful inside and out. A woman above every other.

And she'd chosen him.

Creator Father had brought them together, and as He'd said of His creation in the very first days—this was good.

When they reached White Owl, Caleb touched his arm, placing Lola's hand in his.

White Owl looked at the man. He'd been a good brother to Lola, to them both. No one could ever replace Yagaiki, but Caleb was a gift from Creator Father too. A reminder of His love.

Caleb gave a simple nod, then moved around to stand on their other side.

White Owl turned his focus to Lola, threading their fingers together. The way she looked at him made his chest burn. The love in her eyes matched his own.

With all his strength, for the rest of his days, he would make her feel his love.

And wherever Creator Father took them, the adventure would be far sweeter with this woman by his side.

Did you enjoy White Owl and Lola's story? I hope so!
Would you take a quick minute to leave a review where you purchased the book?
It doesn't have to be long. Just a sentence or two telling what you liked about the story!

~

To receive a free book and get updates when new Misty M. Beller books release, go to https://mistymbeller.com/freebook

And here's a peek at the next book in the series, *Calm in the Mountain Storm*:

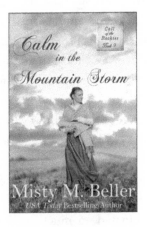

CHAPTER ONE

EARLY WINTER, 1832
FUTURE IDAHO TERRITORY

A warning bell clanged through Elise Turner's body. Something didn't feel right.

The winter wind swept through the valley, and she pulled her buffalo coat tighter. She strained to make out details of the lodges ahead. Were she and her brother too far away to hear sounds of the children who normally played on the land near the camp? Perhaps. But she should be able to see figures moving among the dwellings now.

She glanced over at Ben, who rode astride his gelding. "Does something seem off to you?"

They rode at least a minute farther as Ben studied the Salish village intently. A glance behind showed their companions, White Owl and Lola, also staring at their destination.

"It does seem quiet." Though Ben's voice held its usual measured tone, his words sped up the thud of her heartbeat.

"Do you think visitors have come? Is that why everything is so still?" Lola spoke just loud enough for them all to hear, then her voice softened as she murmured something to her husband.

As Lola reached over and took their tiny babe from White Owl, the child's little fussing sounds drifted forward. Elise's heart squeezed. Little Anna was only two months old now—or two moons, as the natives said it. Either way, she was the perfect age to cuddle. White Owl had kept the cradleboard secured to his chest during most of their day's ride, but he must be handing their daughter off to his wife in case he needed to protect them from possible danger ahead.

White Owl participated so much in the babe's care. Who would imagine that an Indian brave would change soiled nappies as often as his wife did? The white fathers Elise knew didn't do such a thing. Her own pa had been present with his children more than many men in their community, taking one or two at a time along when he visited the sick or ailing in their parish. But he'd left care of the babes to mama and the rest of the girls. Seeing White Owl sweetly cradle little Anna always brought an ache to her chest.

As Lola slipped her arms through the straps on the cradle board, White Owl rode up on Ben's other side. His voice dropped so low, she had to strain to make out his words, still thick with his Shoshone accent. "There is the smell of death ahead. The hungry birds circle above."

Even as his words sent a shiver down her back, her gaze flicked to the sky above the camp. She'd not been mistaken about those turkey vultures. Had the entire village left camp to attend the burial?

A tightness clogged her throat. There had been enough death already. A funeral was the very reason the four of them had gone down to the Nez Perce village a day's ride to the south.

A messenger had come to say Narrow Feet had passed away. Dear Narrow Feet, the first man of his people who'd finally opened his heart to the miracle of God's love and grace. In every village where they stopped to share the gospel, the people there would be resistant until the first one softened. Then one by one, others would come to meet the Lord for themselves. In that Nez Perce camp, Narrow Feet had been the one who turned the tide, the start of the harvest of souls greater than any other camp they'd preached in. Narrow Feet himself had done nearly as much preaching as her and Ben.

And now God had taken him to paradise. A wonderful example of the hope for every believer, but the grief on earth was impossible to ignore.

In this Salish town where they were now returning to, there hadn't yet been that one person to step forward and accept God's grace. Yet perhaps something they'd said had planted a seed, and the harvest had been reaped in their absence.

Lord, let that be the case. Only You can bring forth the harvest of souls. Open their hearts to Your love.

It was the prayer she'd been praying since the first Shoshone village she and Ben had worked in a year and a half ago. The place where they'd met White Owl and been blessed to watch his faith spring to life and grow. He hadn't joined them in their work back then, though they'd invited him to come with them as an interpreter. He and Lola had found them in the Nez Perce village of Narrow Feet, and they'd been so much help—a blessing in too many ways to number. White Owl's skills as an interpreter were invaluable, and Lola's presence as a white woman who'd married into one of the tribes carried a great deal of reassurance for the people.

And little Anna. Having her around doubled the joy in every day. Elise had assisted her mother in raising her own seven younger siblings—there were twelve of them in their family—so one might think she'd be tired of little ones. But they were such a joy, especially while the babes were young enough to be cute and hadn't yet acquired a mischievous streak.

"Elise, you and Lola stay here while White Owl and I ride ahead to see what's happened." Ben's voice held that tone of command he used one he was trying to keep her from running into what he considered danger. He was one of those youngsters she'd helped raise, but he'd always considered himself her protector, even as a boy.

They weren't riding into danger though...this would likely be grief.

Yet he turned his focus to her, brows raised as he waited for her answer.

"All right." If she didn't agree, he would insist she obeyed. She could let the two men go on ahead, then follow a little behind.

As they nudged their horses into a trot, she slowed her mare enough for Lola to ride up alongside.

"I don't like the looks of this." Her friend's voice came out in a hushed singsong as she stroked the soft black fuzz atop Anna's head. "The place looks deserted."

Maybe the entire camp had needed to move on suddenly for some reason. Yet why wouldn't they have taken the lodges?

White Owl and Ben had covered half the distance to the village, but they slowed their horses to walk, studying whatever they saw in the camp.

Elise nudged her mount into a trot. "I'm going to catch up with them."

"Wait. Elise, no." Lola's words faded into the breeze, and Elise sent her friend a slight smile that she hoped offered an apology for ignoring her concerns.

She turned her focus back to the camp, and nothing changed in its appearance as she neared. Not until she reached just past the place the men had slowed.

Was that someone lying on the ground? She reined her mare to a walk and studied the figure. The pressure tightening her chest plunged into her belly, weighting her insides like a mill-stone. The main path between the lodges was not a safe spot for someone to lay. The bright red of the fur wrapped around the figure looked like the one Crying Wolf usually wore. If she'd fallen and injured herself, why would the others leave her, even if they'd been forced to abandon the camp in haste?

Then her gaze caught another form and her throat closed. A sob wrenched through her chest. That little body. Could that be Runs Like the Wind lying prone at the base of his lodge? Then the red marking his buckskin tunic glared at her. She clutched the base of her neck and tore her gaze away.

Lord, what's happened here? Not the child. Not Runs Like the Wind.

She'd stroked the loose hair from his face only last week as he looked up at her and pronounced his name in English. His dark eyes had sparkled with pleasure. Though many of the adults in this camp still eyed her and Ben and Lola and White Owl with distrust, the children let her into their lives and hearts so quickly.

Now she would never see that sweet smile again.

Ben and White Owl had paused at the edge of the village, and she let her gaze move toward them, doing her best to block out Crying Wolf's body that lay just beyond their horses. White Owl dismounted and stepped toward the form, his stride hesitant. He'd likely seen his share of death growing up and trained as a Shoshone warrior. Thank the Lord, he now spoke out for peace...God's peace.

White Owl stepped past Crying Wolf's body, then lifted the flap of the lodge behind her and peered inside. He turned back and spoke to Ben, but Elise couldn't make out his words. Her brother slipped from his horse's back and moved into the village, heading down a different row of huts.

She halted her mare behind the men's horses, keeping the animals as a buffer to block out the sight of the two fallen bodies. She didn't let her gaze lower to either form, but her entire body ached with their loss. Had Runs Like the Wind understood the stories she told of Creator Father who loved him so much He would give his most important possession for the boy? How much could a five-year-old comprehend through sign language and the few words she learned in his tongue?

The cry of a baby jerked her gaze up, and she glanced back at Lola. But her friend had halted her horse too far back for Anna's sounds to be heard this far. And the mewling cry hadn't come from that direction.

She turned back to the camp. Maybe it had been an effect of the wind. She scanned the lodges, her gaze moving around and between them. But as her mind registered more lumps on the ground that looked too much like fallen people, her belly churned. Surely this couldn't be a massacre of the entire village. She'd not let her mind consider that possibility before, and she couldn't stand the thought now. She forced her gaze to the side, toward the thin strip of trees that shaded the river's edge.

A figure there made her breath catch. Her entire body tensed as she focused on him.

An Indian warrior, standing tall as he stared into the empty camp. He stood at least thirty strides away, but even from this distance, she could see the strength in his broad shoulders under the buckskin tunic.

Was he one of the attackers? Maybe he'd stayed behind to make sure none of their victims still lived. Or he might be simply taking a few extra minutes to take pleasure in their victory.

She should scream. Alert Ben and White Owl.

But something about the way the brave stood gave her pause. He didn't puff out his chest or raise a bloody knife in triumph. As the wind brushed loose hair from his face, his outline spoke of grief. Maybe even loneliness.

He held something in his left arm. She focused on the spot. A blanket? It was gray with bright red accents.

An infant's cry sounded, the same tone as before but louder.

Her heart hiccupped at the same moment the warrior looked down at the blanket in his arms. Had he taken a baby from the village before massacring the other inhabitants? Whose child did he have? Yet even as the question flitted through her mind, recognition flared. That was the blanket Bright Eyes had been so proud of owning to wrap her new baby girl within.

This warrior held Pretty Shield. She started to scream, but the man's gaze lifted from the bundle in his arms and met hers. Locking her in place with his eyes. Even over the distance, their intensity held her fixed. His expression spoke of desperation, not at all the defiant look of victory. Was there a chance he wasn't one of the killers?

Either way, she had to get Pretty Shield away from this man —without the infant being hurt. The only chance to do that was to get him to willingly hand over the child.

She nudged her horse toward them, keeping the mare's gait slow. White Owl and Ben were nearby. If she screamed, they would be at her side in an instant. And she also had the rifle Ben insisted she keep strapped to her saddle when they rode. She would never use it on a person, but it seemed wise to have it in case of attack by a wild animal.

If she needed to, she could aim the gun in this man's direction and make him think she would use it. But first she needed to attempt a peaceable request. Surely he had no use for a baby.

Pretty Shield cried out again, and though the man didn't move his gaze from Elise, he lifted his arm in a gentle bounce, a motion that might soothe a fussy infant. As though he'd held a little one like this before.

"Elise, no!" Ben's voice barked through the air, making her nerves jump at the unexpected sound. Footsteps pounded the ground as her brother must be running toward them.

The brave's attention jerked that direction, and his hand flew to a tomahawk strapped to his side. He jerked the weapon out and raised it before Elise could take in a breath to speak. The Indian began to back away, but that tomahawk was poised to fling.

She spun toward her brother. "Ben, stop!"

Her yell didn't even slow him. But the brave was backing away faster now, gripping little Pretty Shield tighter to his chest. The babe had begun crying in earnest. Was he squeezing too tight or was the child so hungry? Or maybe she sensed the horror that was about to happen here.

Elise had to stop this. Raising her voice to a scream, she infused her sharpest big sister tone. "Ben, stop!"

He slowed, his stride moving from a sprint to a jog as he looked to her. She stretched her palm toward him. "He has a baby." Even if the Indian understood English, that shouldn't make him angry.

Ben finally slowed to a walk as he looked at the stranger, then he seemed to fully understand the situation, and he halted completely. "Who are you?" Her brother's voice was far rougher than usual. No doubt, he would be seeing the images of the dead he'd just witnessed for many days to come.

The man didn't answer. He'd already backed deeper into the trees, and he still held his tomahawk raised to throw. But he looked like he might run instead. Did he have a horse nearby? She slid a look through the woods upriver, but no sign of an animal showed.

Perhaps he would feel less cornered if she asked the questions instead of her brother. If he could even understand her words. She couldn't think of a single sign that would speak what she needed to ask, so she'd have to use English.

She swallowed down the lump in her throat and willed the pounding in her heart to slow as she raised her voice. "Who are you, and what are you doing with Bright Eyes's baby?"

Goes Ahead froze as he studied the white woman. How did she know his wife's name? And that this was her child? Who were these strangers who appeared the same day the entire village was murdered?

In his arms, Pretty Shield's cries grew louder, and he forced his hold to loosen. Perhaps he was holding her too tight. Everything in him wanted to wrap both arms around her and sprint far away from these people. But he couldn't react from fear. These white men had rifles and horses, and he had neither. He couldn't risk his own life or that of his tiny daughter.

He forced himself to stand his ground and meet the woman's gaze. Both his children needed him to live and fight for them. He was the only family they had left, and they were everything to him.

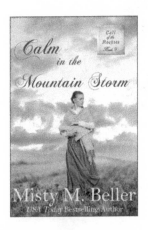

Get CALM IN THE MOUNTAIN STORM at your favorite retailer!

ABOUT THE AUTHOR

Misty M. Beller is a *USA Today* bestselling author of romantic mountain stories, set on the 1800s frontier and woven with the truth of God's love.

Raised on a farm and surrounded by family, Misty developed her love for horses, history, and adventure. These days, her husband and children provide fresh adventure every day, keeping her both grounded and crazy.

Misty's passion is to create inspiring Christian fiction infused with the grandeur of the mountains, writing historical romance that displays God's abundant love through the twists and turns in the lives of her characters.

Sharing her stories with readers is a dream come true for Misty. She writes from her country home in South Carolina and escapes to the mountains any chance she gets.

Connect with Misty at www.MistyMBeller.com

ALSO BY MISTY M. BELLER

Call of the Rockies

Freedom in the Mountain Wind

Hope in the Mountain River

Light in the Mountain Sky

Courage in the Mountain Wilderness

Faith in the Mountain Valley

Honor in the Mountain Refuge

Peace in the Mountain Haven

Grace on the Mountain Trail

Calm in the Mountain Storm

Brides of Laurent

A Warrior's Heart

A Healer's Promise

A Daughter's Courage

Hearts of Montana

Hope's Highest Mountain

Love's Mountain Quest

Faith's Mountain Home

Texas Rancher Trilogy

The Rancher Takes a Cook

The Ranger Takes a Bride

The Rancher Takes a Cowgirl

Wyoming Mountain Tales

A Pony Express Romance

A Rocky Mountain Romance

A Sweetwater River Romance

A Mountain Christmas Romance

The Mountain Series

The Lady and the Mountain Man

The Lady and the Mountain Doctor

The Lady and the Mountain Fire

The Lady and the Mountain Promise

The Lady and the Mountain Call

This Treacherous Journey

This Wilderness Journey

This Freedom Journey (novella)

This Courageous Journey

This Homeward Journey

This Daring Journey

This Healing Journey